PERSONA

ALSO BY

GENEVIEVE VALENTINE

x x x x x x x

THE GIRLS AT THE KINGFISHER CLUB

PERSONA

GENEVIEVE VALENTINE

SAGA PRESS

LONDON SYDNEY **NEW YORK** TORONTO NEW DELHI

SAGA PRESS

An imprint of Simon & Schuster, Inc.

1230 Avenue of the Americas, New York, NY 10020

First Saga Press hardcover edition March 2015

SAGA PRESS and colophon are trademarks of Simon & Schuster, Inc.

For information about special discounts for bulk purchases, please contact Simon & Schuster Special Sales at 1-866-506-1949 or business@simonandschuster.com.

The Simon & Schuster Speakers Bureau can bring authors to your live event. For more information or to book an event, contact the Simon & Schuster Speakers Bureau at 1-866-248-3049 or visit our website at www.simonspeakers.com.

The text for this book is set in Vendetta.

Manufactured in the United States of America

10 9 8 7 6 5 4 3 2 1

Library of Congress Cataloging-in-Publication Data

Valentine, Genevieve.

Persona / Genevieve Valentine. — First edition.

pages ; cm

Summary: "In a world where diplomacy has become celebrity, a young ambassador survives an assassination attempt and must join with an undercover paparazzo in a race to save her life, spin the story, and secure the future of her young country in this near-future political thriller."—Provided by publisher.

ISBN 978-1-4814-2512-4 (hardcover) — ISBN 978-1-4814-2514-8 (eBook)

1. Ambassadors—Fiction. 2. Paparazzi—Fiction. 3. Political fiction. I. Title.

PS3622.A436P47 2015 813'.6—dc23 2014027960

PERSONA

SUYANA SAPAKI PERSONAL ITINERARY
[Classified]

8:00 a.m.	Breakfast
8:30 a.m.	UARC local news briefing [Suyana, Magnus]
9:00 a.m.	~~Rewrite speech for 9:30 a.m. appointment~~ Continue local news briefing [Suyana, Magnus] —SS
9:30 a.m.	Breakfast Event: "P.O.L.Y.G.L.O.T. World Education Foundation" (Your speech has been cut in half; they brought in France at request of press. See above editing session. —MS)
10:30 a.m.	Roll call in chambers
11:00 a.m.	Vote on Prop. 16-SL (The IA is voting Yes; vote is preapproved. —MS)
11:30 a.m.	Lunch with Kipa Forsyth [F, New Zealand]
12:00 p.m.	Global news briefing [Suyana, Magnus]
12:30 p.m.	Nothing currently scheduled (Note that Grace Charles [F, United Kingdom] is hosting an informal event at her flat in the afternoon and has extended an open invitation. Suggest you attend, if they'll have you. —MS) Noted. —SS
12:30 p.m.	~~Walk. SS~~ (Canceled. —MS)
1:30 p.m.	Dress for social call
2:00 p.m.	Car service for social call
2:30 p.m.	Social call
6:00 p.m.	Dress for cocktail event
6:30 p.m.	Cocktail event: South American Press Appreciation Reception (Speech approved. —MS)
8:30 p.m.	Dinner (The reservation is for four, in case afternoon social call goes well or the Press Appreciation Reception yields company. —MS)
11:00 p.m.	End of day

1

The International Assembly audience hall was half-empty—
too empty, Suyana might have said, in her first year there,
when she was still surprised by the distance between good
public relations and good politics. Now, looking across so
many empty seats just made her heavy to the bones.

"Georgia," the proctor called. "Germany. Ghana. Gibraltar."

Missed opportunity, Suyana thought, every time the
proctor's eyes fell on an empty chair. An open vote was one
of the rare times Faces pretended at politics. You were voting
the way you were told, but even pretending was something,
and she couldn't imagine giving it up.

The rest of your life was photo shoots and PSAs and

school visits, and saying what your handler told you to say, and going to parties where you tried desperately to look like you belonged amid a sea of other Faces who were higher on the guest list than you were.

Suyana put up with the rest of it because three or four times a year, she got to raise her hand and be counted. And today was a vote, and only half were here.

Some—the ones who ranked above her on guest lists—didn't bother. Some feared what would happen if they did the wrong thing in front of the Big Nine, and their handlers had advised them to steer clear.

Her stomach twisted.

"They might as well just decide without us and inform us how we voted by mail," she muttered.

Magnus said without looking over, "Try to sound professional, please, on the incredibly slim chance a reporter has a camera on you."

No chance. The United Amazonian Rainforest Confederation had only been interesting three years ago, when the outpost got blown to pieces. Cameras had watched her for six weeks, until some other story broke.

That was before Magnus had been installed; she suspected he'd have worked harder to keep her in the public eye.

She pulled the day's agenda into her lap, and picked the corners of the page off one at a time, where no one could see.

Magnus glanced over, said nothing.

In the sea of middle-aged handlers always conferring just out of camera range, Magnus looked more like a Face—tall, slender, fair, with a sharp expression—and she suspected he'd washed out from IA training, once upon a time. Just as well—he cast glances at the Big Nine as if he couldn't wait to cut himself free of her. Diplomats couldn't be so nakedly ambitious.

Little pieces of paper came off in her hands.

She couldn't blame him; sometimes people had different loyalties than they were supposed to.

Smooth it over, she reminded herself. Keep an even keel. Don't let anyone catch you out. Some things you can't afford.

"I'm just nervous," she said, softly.

It was true, but it was also what Magnus wanted to hear from her. Sure enough, he looked over.

"Understandable," he said, high praise from him. "I have the rental."

The rental was a necklace that was supposed to make her look fashionable, prosperous, alluring. Suyana thought it was useless, since her owning a bib of semiprecious stones would seem either openly false or a monstrous luxury depending on how much you knew about UARC economics, but Magnus had set his mind on it, and she wasn't going to let it matter.

"Not sure it will do much. In *Closer* last year, he said he liked natural beauties."

Magnus raised an eyebrow. "How cosmopolitan."

"Iceland," the proctor called. "India."

"I don't like the non-compete clause," Magnus said. "Six months is restrictive. They're hoping to leverage the re-up option in case the public likes you." From his tone of voice, that wasn't likely.

"Exclusivity ends the day the contract ends. They have the physical clause; you can't enforce a non-compete on that. If he doesn't want me to go elsewhere, he can make his offer alongside everyone else."

He frowned. Three years on, he still got surprised whenever she slipped and got honest. (Most of the time Suyana wanted to strangle him. She measured her success as a diplomat by how little he caught on.)

"Japan," the proctor called, and at the Big Nine table, far down the chamber ahead of her, the Face from Japan raised his hand.

"Suyana," Magnus said, as careful as with any stranger he was trying to persuade. "We're not in a place to dictate changes. We're lucky they're interested. After what happened—"

"I remember what happened."

There was a little silence.

She missed Hakan, a knife of grief sliding between

her ribs. She held her breath, like it could bring him back from the dead. Smooth expression, she thought. Show nothing. Be nothing.

"Norway," the proctor called, with no answer.

Only six of the Big Nine had deigned to appear. Grace, the best of the lot, was without her handler—she always looked more eligible sitting alone. Grace was number two on *Intrigue* magazine's Most Eligible Faces list for the fourth year in a row.

Suyana had already planned an attack of nerves so she'd miss Grace's party. She was wary of open invitations; felt too much like charity sometimes.

Norway's seats were empty. They were voting on some potential additions to the IA's Human Rights Declaration, but apparently Martine didn't think that was something that needed her attention.

("You should go talk to her," Magnus said once at an afternoon reception, and Suyana said, "Yes, nothing raises your social stock like being ignored by your betters.")

Ethan Chambers, the American Face, had sent one of his assistants as a proxy; the Big Nine had enough staff to have them in two places at once.

At least there she knew the reason why.

Ethan Chambers was sitting in a boutique hotel a few miles away, waiting to meet her and sign the contract for a six-month public relationship. There would also be discussion of the terms of the physical clause; they were rare enough that they required careful debate, which meant everyone was preparing for several awkward hours. Still, you did what you had to, to get someone's attention—the physical clause was the reason the United States had taken her offer seriously.

Suyana suspected the American team thought that if Ethan got her in bed, she'd get emotionally involved, and be easier to pressure with PR fallout whenever they wanted the UARC to fall in line.

Everyone could dream, she supposed.

"New Zealand," the proctor called, and a few rows in front of her, Kipa raised her hand for each count of the amendments. Each time, it was steady and sure, and Kipa locked her elbow as if to make sure her vote was counted. Suyana tried not to smile. Her turn was coming soon enough, and she didn't want to know what she looked like when she was pretending she made a difference.

After she'd exercised her duties, there would be lunch with Ethan. After lunch, they'd start mapping out the first place they'd be caught together "accidentally."

After that—

"United Amazonian Rainforest Confederation," the proctor called.

Suyana smiled for the cameras, raised her hand to be counted.

2

Daniel wished he'd stolen a camera he actually knew how to use.

He huddled deeper into the restaurant alley and pried the long end of a paper clip into the lens assembly, trying to loosen whatever had jammed the thing in the first place before the sedan showed up and he missed his chance to shoot Suyana. His hands were shaking a little.

Suyana Sapaki was a risk for a shoot on spec. She'd barely escaped being burned out three years ago; she was on the verge of a comeback, but a verge is a tricky thing to measure. Too late and you're drowned in the tide, too early and the pictures go for nothing and get used as archive footage without royalties whenever they finally do something interesting.

But the alley was perfectly positioned across the street from the swank hotel where Ethan Chambers, Face of the United States, was waiting to meet Suyana Sapaki on business unknown. The bellboy Daniel bribed said Ethan had been there since yesterday while his empty car drove all over town.

The lens assembly slid back into place, and Daniel settled behind a garbage can—the poor man's tripod—to focus before Suyana's car showed up.

He hoped it was worth what he'd spent on intel to catch negotiations between the US Face and what Daniel suspected was his girlfriend-to-be. He couldn't afford to go home.

The sedan turned the corner—a cab, not one from the IA fleet. Daniel braced his hands. They still shook a little before a great shot. (It was embarrassing—he was twenty-two, not twelve, he knew how to take pictures—but sometimes the thrill got the better of him.)

Magnus got out first. He was the UARC's new handler, a pro from some Scandinavian country they'd brought in to help spin the disaster, and he looked like a man who was used to getting out of messes clean.

Magnus scanned the square for a moment before he reached back into the car, to call Suyana out.

*[Submission 35178, Frame 7: Magnus Samuelsson
standing beside a black sedan sitting around the corner
from the front entrance to the Chanson Hotel. Subject in
profile and three-quarters length, hand extended into the
backseat of the car, looking at something out of frame.]*

Weird, Daniel thought, risking a glance up from the viewfinder. Magnus didn't seem the type to get swept up in scenery, and it wasn't as though Ethan Chambers would be standing with flowers at the balcony to greet the girl he might be about to contract to date.

He didn't know much about most of the IA handlers— you weren't supposed to, that's why countries had Faces, to give you something to look at—but something seemed off. Had they fought in the car? Was Magnus just cautious? Had he arranged for official nation-affiliated photographers to catch the first moments of budding romance, and Daniel was going to be without an exclusive after all this?

But then Suyana stepped out of the car, and Daniel forgot everything in the queasy thrill of a scoop.

*[Submission 35178, Frame 18: Suyana Sapaki (Face UARC),
sliding out of the backseat of a sedan. Large necklace—appears
genuine (ID and trail of ownership TK). Face three-quarters,
turned to the hotel. Has not taken Samuelsson's hand.]*

Daniel had, once or twice in his research for this, questioned why Suyana had been considered the best option for the Face of the UARC. She was Peruvian, and the Brazilian contingent had given her flak for it—they were a much bigger slice of that pie, and a Quechua was playing even harder against the numbers, unless you were going after diversity points. She was a little stocky in a world that liked its Faces tall and thin, a little hard around the eyes in an organization that prized girls who could fawn when the cameras were going. Even from here it looked like she was suffering a punishment. No way that was true—if she could get Ethan to sign on the dotted line, it was a PR coup the UARC could only dream of.

But her brown skin and knotted black hair and sharp eyes made a decent picture when the light hit her, and she moved with more purpose than Daniel saw from a lot of IA girls. (Wasn't much purpose for her to have, except look good and do as she was told. Handlers did the real work. Faces just made it look sharp to the masses. Though nobody wanted a Face getting ideas, as they'd reminded him plenty back home.)

Once the car pulled away, Magnus looked Suyana over with the focus of an auctioneer. He lifted his chin as if inviting her to do the same; Suyana stared through him and didn't move. Magnus straightened the collar of her shirt, tweaked one of the careless gems on her necklace so that it lay right side up against her collarbone.

Daniel raised his eyebrow into the viewfinder, took a few shots as fast as he could.

He'd seen backstage prep on the Korean Face, Hae Soo-jin, when he was still apprenticing as a licensed photographer. Most of it looked like grooming animals for auction, if you were being honest. This was something different; some message passing back and forth through a necklace that was laughably out of place on her.

Suyana glanced at Magnus for a moment with a frown that was gone before Daniel could catch it. Then she turned her head, as if she was used to being altered by people she didn't look at.

That was about right. The ideal combination of *hanbok* and national designers a Face should wear to present the correct ratio of tradition and modernism had been a hot topic at home when he left. The news had a segment on it at least once a week. Historians were weighing in; fashion-industry insiders staged demonstrations. Hae Soo-jin hadn't been called on for an opinion. Decision making happened before anything ever reached them. You could measure the length of a Face's career by seeing how good they were at agreeing with other people's outcomes.

But Suyana had looked at Magnus so strangely. Maybe it bothered her to know how far on the sidelines she stood.

[*Submission 35178, Frame 39: Magnus Samuelsson,
back to the camera (identified in Frames 1–13).
Facing the camera, Suyana Sapaki. Samuelsson has
his hand extended toward Sapaki's elbow.
Sapaki looking off-frame (object of gaze unknown),
hands in pockets. No acknowledgment.*]

"It doesn't matter," Suyana said. "He'll know it's not mine." Her voice floated a little around the square before it settled on Daniel.

"We're impressing an ally, not a jeweler," said Magnus. "You need all the help you can get. No use looking shabby first thing. Are you ready to be charming?"

She looked right at Magnus, and Daniel flinched at her expression (murderer, he thought wildly, like he was watching a movie) and wished for a concurrent video function so he could try to capture what the hell was even going on.

Then she blinked, and her eyes softened, and her smile broke wide and white across her face. "Of course," she said, in a voice that sounded barely hers. "Are you ready to chaperone?"

Magnus's jaw twitched—surprised, maybe, or put out—and he looked back toward the street like he was thinking of making a run for it. "Let's go."

Suyana pushed her shoulders back, licked her lips, and headed for the front door of the hotel like she was on her way to a prison sentence. Magnus followed a little behind; most handlers did when their Faces were onstage. There was no good in the policymakers hogging the spotlight.

Daniel should have kept better track of how the light was moving; shadows giving way to the flood of sunlight across the white hotel made him blink into the viewfinder, and he took pictures by reflex as he waited for his eyes to adjust.

He was still waiting when the gunshot rang out.

All the sound was sucked out of the square for a second in the wake of the shot. His finger never stopped moving. He hoped against all luck that he'd managed to catch the moment the bullet hit. If there was a bullet.

There were publicity stunts like this, sometimes, when someone needed the sympathy. They made front pages, no matter how horrible and obvious a ploy it was.

As the shutter clicked, the sound washed back—people shouting behind the closed door of the restaurant, Magnus staggering back with one arm out toward Suyana, casting an eye around the rooftops (why wasn't he in front of her? Why wasn't he protecting his charge?).

And Suyana was scrambling up from the ground, favoring one leg but already trying to bolt for the nearest cover. She looked young, in her terror, but her jaw was set—she would live, if she could.

Too bad he'd missed that shot, Daniel thought as he pocketed his memory card and shoved the camera into the trash. He wasn't going to get arrested for unauthorized photography, and he sure as hell wasn't going to get shot in some publicity stunt. She was coming his way, and he knew when to exit the scene.

But as Suyana dove toward the alley, there was another shot. She staggered and cried out—once, sharp—and he saw she had a bloody hand pressed to her left arm, that now the right leg of her jeans was blooming dark with blood.

He had to get out of there.

But she was running for the alley—lurching, really. She wasn't going to make it in time to avoid a kill shot if it came, if this wasn't a stunt. It might be a stunt. Either way, snaps didn't get involved. The hair on his arms was standing up.

Magnus was shouting, somewhere out of sight (the hotel?). A car engine flared to life (the cab?).

Suyana was gasping for breath.

You're a sucker, Daniel thought, you're a sucker, don't you dare, but by then he was already out in the square, scooping her under her good shoulder.

There was a bottle-cap pop from somewhere far away that he knew must be a bullet. Then they were running a three-legged race into the safety of the alley.

He let go as soon as she was in the shadows, but she

caught hold of his elbow with more force than he'd have guessed she could manage. The tips of her fingers were rough; they caught on his sleeve.

"Save it," he said, eyeing the street on the far side of the alley, to make sure it was clear when he ran for it, but then he made a mistake and looked back at her.

Either she was a damn good actress or she was tougher than he'd thought. Her mouth was pulled tight with panic, but she looked at him like she was sizing him up.

"Thanks," she said, and somehow it was a demand for information, which was funny coming from someone who was bleeding in two places.

He couldn't believe he'd gone out there. This was a handler's job, if the shooting was even real—where the hell was Magnus?—and not one damn second of this was his business except behind a lens. This story had played out, and he was in enough trouble. He'd come back for the camera later. Maybe.

He said, "I have to go."

Tires screeched around the corner, and from somewhere came the echo of footsteps, and the hair on Daniel's neck stood up—his heart was in his throat, this was amateur hour, this was chaos.

Who knew this was happening today besides me? he wondered, from some suspicion he didn't want to examine.

Suyana swayed, braced herself on her good arm against the wall like a sprinter on the starting line, her eyes fixed on the far end of the alley. There were footsteps, voices shouting. They're looking for us, Daniel realized, and his blood went cold.

Suyana looked up at him, and for a moment he remembered the footage from a few years back, right after terrorists hit the UARC, and she'd bored holes at any camera that crossed her like she was daring them to ask.

She said, "Run."

3

He'd cased the neighborhood—it would have been a rookie mistake to go into something like that without an exit ready— so for thirty seconds he knew where he was going, and it was just another practice run.

For thirty seconds he focused on the uneven pavement under his feet, on avoiding the tables that littered the sidewalk, on cutting across tricky intersections in a way that made it hard for, say, a police car to follow you.

They saw few people, thank goodness—a tabac owner who peered at them through the window, an old woman who saw them and startled, a musician who got one look at them and spun on his heels the other way, his black bag banging against his back in his haste. Otherwise, for thirty seconds, Daniel could think.

He'd mapped out routes across three bridges, and angled toward the busiest (Notre-Dame tourists were easy to disappear into, if he could just get there), and they were on a narrow side street nearly at the main route to Pont Saint Louis when the panic set in.

It didn't even feel like panic, really—his knees just buckled between one step and the next like all the muscle had fallen out of them. He stumbled, reached for the nearest wall to keep from falling over.

Suyana pulled up beside him, and turned to keep her bad shoulder out of sight of the rest of the street. It brought them face-to-face. She was breathing hard, and her jaw was clenched like she was trying not to be sick.

Her eyes were wide and dark, but her eyebrows were fixed carefully without expression. Absently he thought about Halloween, streets full of masks.

She was losing blood. She couldn't run for much longer. He hoped she wasn't thinking of asking for his help to get to a hospital; things were bad enough without her trying some teary-eyed bid for sympathy the way IA girls did on TV when they were asking for humanitarian aid.

There were no tears. She looked him over a second, said, "If you can't keep going, I'll go on alone."

He nearly laughed. What diplomat talked this way to someone they'd barely met? What Face talked this way to anyone at all?

"I'm not the one who's been shot."

She flinched and looked over her shoulder as if people would hear and come running. "I'll make it."

"Make it where? You're bleeding all over your shirt."

She shrugged with her good shoulder, gritted her teeth against the pain. "I'm short on supplies and no one's offered me a coat."

Well, he wasn't about to do it just because she'd needled him. But he might have to change his appearance if things caught up to him, and it wouldn't matter much where his coat went after that—on her or in the garbage.

Under all the sounds of the crowd and his pulse banging against his ears, he was listening for someone following them. He'd outrun trouble before, plenty. It was always a matter of hearing them before they saw you.

He ran a hand through his hair as an excuse to look behind them. Two silhouettes passed, paused, and moved on. It could be anybody.

Suyana said, "I'll give you this necklace if you can get me to Montmartre."

That was interesting. At least it wasn't a sympathy ploy. Bald barter was unusual, but more honest.

"That thing looks like a fake," he said, shrugged. "Pass."

She looked at him, said, "You know it's not."

Suddenly all his breath was missing. He blinked, licked his lips.

There was a flicker of a smile at one corner of her mouth, but it vanished. "You were already in the alley when they shot me. You heard us."

When they shot me, she said, calm as if she were talking about cameras. But she wasn't entirely in control. Her face was sallow, and the hand pressed against her arm was starting to shake.

He didn't like how this was going. Maybe it was better to cut things off at the knees.

He leaned a little closer, pitched his voice low. "Maybe I was in on it."

She tensed up when he moved toward her, but there was no surprise, no moment of horror setting in. The idea must have already occurred to her. Not a lot of trust among diplomats.

But she was still looking at him, and she narrowed her eyes a little before she said, "Then why did you panic?"

Daniel wished he'd picked a dumber Face to follow.

It occurred to him to point out that this could all be a ploy to slow her down—it's not like he'd panicked, really, it was just that he had stopped to consider—but if she really believed that, she'd have run for it five turns back, going it alone halfway across the bridge by now. He could see her leaving a blood trail straight through the cathedral and out the other side.

Someone was coming up behind them—lightweight, carrying metal, in a hurry.

Her eyes went wide as saucers. She backed up two steps, grimacing against the pain, and turned to bolt.

"Hold it," Daniel hissed.

A moment later, a teenager raced past them, clutching a familiar camera tight by the strap as it rattled against his fist. (Daniel knew exactly what making a break for it with a stolen camera sounded like.)

After the kid rounded the corner, Suyana held still longer than she had to. Her eyes unfocused for a second; she blinked slowly, took a breath that sounded like it cost her. He wondered if this was one of the things they taught you to do— if diplomacy was half smiles and firm handshakes and the other half was pretending you were about to be sick to get out of a bad situation.

"Okay, I'm not in on it, you got me," he said, just to say something, and smiled just to have something for his face to do.

If he was lucky, she thought he was a busboy who went out for a smoke and got caught in the crossfire. If she figured out he was a snap, he was in trouble. For all the time they spent in the public eye, Faces didn't like the idea they were being watched, and the IA-approved national photographers didn't stand for competitive press.

And if she left him, he'd lose this chance. The next he'd hear about her would be on the news, with IA press taking portraits of her in blood-spattered clothes as she emerged from the alleys of Paris, having escaped the gunmen she'd hired for show. Or the gunmen were real, and she'd be dead. Either way, he'd miss the story.

"You need a hospital," he said.

She shook her head. "I'm fine. We need to get going."

Every sentence that came out of her mouth made her stranger. "Well, then let's call"—he bit off *your handler*, he wasn't supposed to know that—"someone."

"My handler can wait," she said, the way she'd talked about the necklace—sharp, angry at him for playing dumb.

He shrugged off his jacket and draped it across her shoulders. As he moved closer she tensed, but he stood beside her as though they were a couple, wrapped an arm around her to help hold her up. She was solid as stone under his hand. He could feel her fingers still pressing tight against the wound. She seemed awkward more than afraid, as if it had been a long time since she'd hugged anyone.

"We'll have to keep to the small streets if you can't run," he said.

She tested her right leg. Her lips thinned. "Fine."

Wherever she was going, she was damn fixed on getting there. If he could manage this story, it would be the making of him. He was smarter than he'd been when he'd fled home. He could wring the truth out of Suyana Sapaki.

If his heart was still pounding, that made sense. If the worst of his panic had vanished while he was talking to her, he didn't think about it.

"What is there in Montmartre, anyway?"

She smiled. "I'll show you."

It was the smile she'd given Magnus, wide and false, when she was right in the middle of a lie. Oh, he thought, we'll see about that.

"All right," he said. He squeezed her shoulder against the flow of blood. The fabric under his fingertips was damp.

They turned onto the avenue, ducked into the narrow street across the way, and headed north, where the sun was just beginning to set on Montmartre.

4

Suyana weighed her options.

It was difficult—she was light-headed from bleeding, and a stranger was steering her through the streets of Paris as fast as she could manage, which was more frightening than being shot at.

When you signed up for the IA, they told you over and over to think about the possibility, just to get you used to the idea that someday you'd be facing down the barrel of a gun. They never told you to expect help; not something you got much of.

She was letting it happen because she needed to get to Montmartre more than she needed to break free, just now. She had to make it to the apartment without bleeding to death on foreign soil. The IA would have a field day with that.

Maybe not. The IA might might have ordered it; maybe writing up her untimely end on the soft-focus streets of Paris was just what they were hoping for.

It was terrifying just to imagine it, but you couldn't shrink from the truth if it illuminated what needed to be done. It was the IA, or the Americans, or Magnus acting on orders from home.

(She'd made the list as soon as she registered what was happening. Then she'd thought, I have to get north and warn them, with a twinge like homesickness. Then pain.)

If it was the Americans or her own country, it would be messy. Her own country she might be able to handle; accusing the Americans would mean some serious diplomatic incidents for not a lot of gain—the Americans had a way of avoiding consequences.

If the IA had moved against her, she was probably a dead woman, but she fought it. You rose to the need. She took a breath, counted her pulse like Hakan had taught her when she was thirteen and hadn't even seen the floor of the IA yet.

("Some of them are born into this. They'll see weaknesses—they're bred on arguments. Think about whether your anger is productive."

"My anger's why you brought me here," she'd said.

He'd smiled. He had laugh lines, which surprised her:

How could you be happy inside a machine? But he was. "Then make the most of your chances," he'd said, "so you live long enough to be back home again."

It was good advice; advice he hadn't followed.)

Suyana had lost the advantage of anonymity to the stranger, which was too bad. Even when it was necessary, it was a shame to give first. But you had to weigh the cost of anything, and it had been more important to take his measure than to feign ignorance. Now she knew two things: what he looked like when he was lying, and what he looked like when he was truly surprised.

"You all right?" he asked. They were nearing an enormous intersection.

She glanced toward the pavement at their feet. "How much blood am I trailing?"

"I'm surprised you have any left," he said. His jaw was set, and he didn't look down.

That meant he'd already looked at her and she hadn't seen it. No good. She needed to stay sharp. She could lay out her options later, when she had any options besides Live or Mistake.

"I just need to make it to the stairs on rue Foyatier," she said. Her voice was light—she was dizzy—and she didn't like it. To make it come off more girlish than weak, she gave him half a smile, as if the stairs were a whim in which he'd be kind enough to indulge her, and later they'd go out for coffee and laugh about it. Grace used it sometimes, when she was in front of the full Assembly.

He flexed his fingers around her shoulder absently, the sort of reflex you had when you remembered a hidden weapon you were planning to use. "So you wanted to jog your way up to the church?"

It was a false question, just filling space.

The first time she'd really met Ethan—a party at Terrain— he'd done the same thing, so when he lurched forward with his elbows on his knees and knuckles bumping the table and asked, "So what's it like to live so close to the rainforest?" she thought he knew more than he should.

But he was just a diplomat, trained not to leave empty space in a conversation unless he was trying to intimidate. She'd laughed and explained where she was really from, ghosting her fingers on his knuckles as she sketched the mountains with her hands along the table.

He'd dropped his gaze to her fingers, taken a second too long to answer. Later, she'd wonder if this was the moment she began to think about the contract—the moment he'd been caught off guard, and had considered it quietly without pushing back. It was unexpected; it was promising.

She'd left before he could get restless. (If the Americans had arranged the hit, that would probably answer the question of dating Ethan.)

But Ethan asked empty questions because he had nothing else to say. This one was asking empty questions to distract her.

Thieves, the people who skim across things that way; thieves and people who are lying to you. Fair enough. It wasn't as though any of this had been a humanitarian gesture, and there was no future in it. Even as he'd yanked her out of the line of fire, he had the face of someone who regretted it. This one was out for himself.

She understood. She could handle that.

They were nearly at Foyatier now—she recognized the neighborhood from the pictures in her IA dossier. Almost there, she thought, as if it were home.

She took a breath, counted her pulse, and set about planning the best way to lose him.

A few blocks later he turned them abruptly down a side street—what had he seen? No way anyone could have followed them through this labyrinth in dusk—and she pivoted on her bad leg, grinding her foot into the ground for balance.

There was a burst of pain; her vision clouded. She moved faster, so he couldn't tell anything was wrong.

"We're almost there," he said. "There were just police that way. We're going up the next street."

Good. The last thing she could afford was to be seen by police. They'd send her back to Magnus.

She didn't know where Magnus was when the first shot

came—those memories were muddled. But by the time she was scrambling from the gunfire, she'd seen the little square. Magnus had vanished. No use, trusting some.

It was almost too dark to read by the time they finally reached the stairs.

"You're not going to actually try to climb them, are you?"

She'd take it as a compliment that he thought she still could. "Hang on," she said. "My ankle."

He glanced down and shifted his grip on her shoulders (pain lanced down her arm), but she ignored it and scanned the flat cobbles that framed the stairs until she had what she needed. It was white chalk, hard to see if you weren't looking, and she'd have been in trouble if it rained.

"I don't see your friends." He was setting her down on a bench, more gently than she would have expected.

"They'll be here," she said. "Thank you so much for everything. I need to pay you before you go. Except—I can't reach, sorry." She ducked her head. "You'll have to do it."

She watched his feet. He shifted his weight, moving forward and pulling back. There was a pause that was longer than it should have been. Then his fingers brushed against her neck, and the necklace swung free.

It was a relief; she didn't realize how heavy it had been. When she looked up, she caught a strange expression on his face. She was reminded, just for a second, of Magnus as he'd pushed the last stone along her collarbone so she'd look presentable when she met the Americans.

"Well." He frowned at the necklace, slid it into his pocket. "I can't just go. I wouldn't feel right leaving you. For a tip like this, you should get full service." He gave her a smile like when he'd bullshitted her about what he'd heard in the alley, some old chestnut he knew would work.

He couldn't be serious. Who wouldn't take a prize like that and run? Someone who wasn't in it for the money, she thought, and her fingertips went cold. Who was he?

She'd never had to work to get rid of people—in the IA, it was always work to keep them talking. She had to get him out of the way long enough to disappear.

"Well," she said, "you can wait with me if you feel like being a gentleman."

He took a seat, settled in. She thought about her angle. The place was close enough—three blocks, the marking indicated, three or four, she could walk three or four still. All she needed was to get there, and she'd be taken care of. She'd crawl that far, to be safe.

"So," he said, "what do you think of Paris?"

He wasn't filling the silence now; now he was glancing at her sidelong, and she heard the hundred questions behind the question.

"Lovely city to get shot in," she said.

He laughed once, real and surprised.

She had to put some distance between them. What she had to do now was too dangerous for anyone else, even if she did trust him farther than she could throw him. She closed her eyes, swayed a little (not too much—just closing her eyes made the street spin).

"Shit, hey," he said, one hand on her shoulder. "You have to get these looked at."

"No hospitals," she said, sharp. Hospitals meant police and Magnus, and she couldn't risk either.

He didn't push it, and she wondered if he guessed that she didn't want to make herself known to her handler. Somehow that was worse than anything.

"Are your friends medics, at least?"

Some of them had better be. "Could you—" She looked around the square. "I need water, I'm so dizzy."

There was a moment's hesitation before he nodded—not stupid, this one. "Will you still be here when I get back?"

"No, I'm going to jog the stairs a few times to get the blood going."

He half smiled. "Be right back."

Why she should feel guilty about this, she had no idea. He'd been paid more than enough for his labors. He had to know this was temporary.

He took off at a good clip, dodging tourists who were passing, and ducked into a tabac at the corner. He'd be back in two minutes. Less. She'd have to make a run for it.

She gritted her teeth and lurched off the bench. Her leg was burning, and there was a starry jolt as though she'd been punched in the nose, but she put as much weight on it as she dared, tried to walk normally.

Her jeans were crusted with blood—it was too dark for anyone to tell now, but they'd gone stiff, and scratched the wound with every step. She crossed her arms as if she was cold, wrapped one hand over her sleeve as hard as she could. She hoped the guy had another jacket at home; he was never getting this one back.

Two blocks. She'd made it two blocks. She could make it. She just had to keep an eye out for the right street—they knew who she was, they would have as much to lose as she did. She'd be all right, as soon as she was with them.

Something moved in the corner of her eye.

Tourists, three of them, holding up their phones and taking pictures of the skyline. Harmless, but she couldn't be seen in pictures. She turned away, walked faster. Her head really was swimming—as she squinted up at the street sign, the letters ran together—but she couldn't risk slowing down.

There were footsteps closer behind, moving quickly. She couldn't look behind her—no windows with a good enough reflection. Out of nowhere the thought slammed into her: the stranger's here to finish me off. But it felt hollow, like there wasn't enough blood left for her to really panic.

That's probably for the best, she thought.

Then she passed out.

5

Daniel knew she'd run. He moved fast, carefully not looking at the magazine rack—some Faces had gone to Milan for Fashion Week to support their national designers, and *Closer* had a snap of Philippe Arnaud walking hand in hand with a model. (It was a small picture, and the caption hadn't even bothered to identify the model. Guys usually got away with flings outside the IA—if he wasn't under contract with someone, there wasn't much story there.)

He'd been gone only a couple of minutes, but he wasn't surprised when he turned the corner to an empty bench. She wasn't the type to wait around and debate her options. Still, his throat went tight. The reflex of losing a story, probably. Her necklace was in his pocket, heavy, still warm from her neck.

But he pulled himself together. She couldn't go far in the state she was in. He scanned the thin early-evening crowd for anyone struggling to stay upright.

He saw something move—fall?—and vanish from sight just as two tourists jumped down from the stairs right in front of him, gasping and clutching at each other for balance as they held up their phones to record what they'd descended.

As they passed him (he was edging around them, head down and turned away from the cameras), he saw a pair of shadows kneeling over someone, too far away to distinguish.

There were people still in the streets, he thought— nothing could happen to her, not in front of so many people.

But then one of them was on the phone relaying details, and whatever carrion birds he'd imagined hovering over her became just another pair of tourists calling an ambulance for a stranger.

They reached down (Daniel started moving, they couldn't just start jostling her, something could be broken), but he was too far away and one of them was already holding up Suyana's wrist, saying something to his friend, who repeated it into the phone. Her hand was limp, he could see it even from here. Out cold. Did they know who she was? Had the news gone out about her?

If Daniel had an ounce of sense he'd turn around now,

take what he had to the black market, and try to catch the eye of an agency. A frame of a Face getting shot was enough to go on. He'd get plenty of offers. He closed his hand around the necklace until the stones bit.

Still, it would be a shame not to follow her. The more complete your story, the better the money was. He needed the money; he needed enough to buy himself out of trouble. She would understand, if she knew. She hadn't been home in a long time either.

She hadn't wanted to be taken to a hospital. He could guess why.

The hardest thing was staying out of the way until the ambulance came—those tourists hovered, and they didn't take pictures of themselves with an unconscious woman, but it came close. (Daniel was nearly on top of them by the time the first guy talked the second guy out of it. He vanished around a corner for a little while just in case they'd noticed.)

After the authorities had her it was easier. He was no stranger to tailing someone, and traffic was bad enough that it was no trouble keeping the red van in sight all the way to the hospital.

Daniel stood outside the emergency-room doors as night crept over him, wondering what the hell was happening, and how he was ever going to get to her.

× × × × × × ×

Even if they required a little more groundwork first, Daniel found that the best lies always came in pairs, so they could rest on each other.

For the first round he feigned flower delivery, walking up and down the halls with the ugliest lilies he'd ever seen, peering at room numbers and marking exits for fifteen minutes, until he overheard one of the nurses mention needing blood for "Mlle Dupont" as she passed an orderly.

He couldn't tell if they'd recognized her yet. They'd have called the police, so he'd have that to worry about, but if they knew she was IA, no flower-delivery act was going to cut it. He could rule out sneaking in with a lab coat, too—wherever she was, that floor would be locked.

He glanced at the emergency boards. She was already in a recovery room, so whatever had been necessary to patch her up wasn't serious. Good. Bones splintered under bullets, sometimes. She'd been lucky.

Now he had to get in with her and buy them some time. Not that there was a *them* (there was a him and a story), but you didn't half drag someone to a mysterious meeting place just to give up on your chances. Really, he was her best option. He had no idea where Samuelsson had been when the shooting started. And if anyone else showed up looking for her, he was pretty certain it would be bad news. If she was leaving, best she leave with him.

He set the bouquet in the corner of an empty nurse's station where he could, in an emergency, come back for them and pretend he'd just been in the men's room. They were safe—no one would want to claim these. Then he went back outside, to gather courage and steal a coat.

He'd known people back home who could really run cons like this—they got into parties, press conferences, hotel suites. It had been for money or blackmail, most of the time, but a skill was a skill.

He understood being shameless (of course he did), but he'd never been able to mirror the people who pulled it off. They always acted as if whatever they were asking for was the dullest, most necessary chore in the world. He could spin a decent story, but every once in a while he'd overdo it. The trick was in the boredom.

He could stop letting this matter. He could stop letting Suyana Sapaki have any hold over him at all. Why should he care? Once you cared, you had something to lose. This was just the most necessary chore.

He came in through the front entrance, stolen coat on, jaw set, not looking left or right. He'd watched enough footage of the IA to know how people acted when they knew they could move mountains. The few people in the waiting room glanced over from the TV, just for a moment, like people do when someone important passes by.

He went up to the reception station and rested the tips of his fingers on the desk, leaning in just slightly, the way handlers sometimes did when they were taking something off the record.

"I'm here for your nameless mademoiselle," he said in deliberately awful French, half an order, half bored out of his mind.

The administrator started with recognition and blinked before she could summon the lie. "I'm sorry, Monsieur, I don't know who you mean."

"Good," he said in English, "and we appreciate your discretion. Now tell me where she is."

She cleared her throat, glanced at the computer. "Sir, I'm very sorry, I don't—"

"All right. I was warned about a lack of critical thinking, but I was hoping you'd surprise me. I'm not here because I like leaving in the middle of a state meal. I need to see her so we can clean up this mess before half of Europe's IA Peacekeeping forces descend on Paris. Now, please."

She frowned and looked him over. He wondered if it was too late, and Magnus had come in while he was gone, and Suyana would be going right back into the sights of whoever had tried to kill her.

Don't care, he thought, don't care, don't care.

"Do you have ID?"

Withering, he said, "In my division, it wouldn't be my real ID anyway, would it?"

Behind him, Daniel heard a familiar voice (on television, he realized, just after his heart dropped into his stomach).

"—under fire," Magnus Samuelsson was saying. From the stone silence that followed, Daniel couldn't tell if it was a studio recording or a press conference, and he didn't dare turn around.

"Today," Samuelsson went on, "Suyana Sapaki suffered a grievous injury at the hands of parties unknown, here on Paris soil."

Daniel felt a little sick. But the receptionist had blanched, so he raised his eyebrows at her, spread his hands. What did he care if the IA descended? It wasn't his hospital.

"Just a moment," she said, reaching for her phone.

He glanced at the television. He wanted to know what the man's face looked like when he was giving a party line like this. He'd probably been in on it.

Samuelsson looked utterly calm, the front of one of his three-piece Impressive Suits utterly smooth, and he was reading off a piece of paper to a room of stone-faced photographers wearing their national colors and dutifully recording.

"Due to the nature of her injuries," Samuelsson read, "Ms. Sapaki's prognosis is, at the moment, unknown."

Then there was an expression he couldn't place, just for a second, before her face closed shut like it always did when cameras were on her.

It occurred to him that she might have been making alternate plans, and she'd call out to the nurses any second to get rid of the guy she'd blackmailed and who wouldn't leave her alone.

But she didn't call out. She didn't say anything. She watched him, eyes narrowed, braced for the worst.

A lot of questions fell out in front of him, any of them worth a hundred thousand euros if he got an answer. Who shot you? Do you think Magnus Samuelsson knows who shot you? Who's the friend you never met? Are you so short on friends that you're surprised I came back?

Are you all right? Do you know what's happened to you, while you were in here alone?

He settled on, "There's something you need to see."

This channel was predictable—they were replaying the whole statement with inconvenient breaks so studio commentators who had no idea what was happening could talk with great authority about it.

Suyana watched the introductions with no expression. If Samuelsson had arranged to have her killed, it must not upset her much. Maybe they'd worked together after all, setting up

He glanced up into the camera, just for a moment, then back at the paper. He kept going, and there was a murmur through the audience, but as Samuelsson was talking the receptionist was hanging up and telling Daniel a room number and waving him through a door that needed a buzzer, and Daniel was trying to keep his voice even as he asked her as archly as possible to let him know when the police had arrived, and his pulse was so loud in his ears he probably wouldn't have heard whatever Samuelsson had to say.

[*ID 29963, Frame 7: Daniel Park in black coat, walking through security doors of Hôpital François du Lac, looking over his shoulder at broadcast of Magnus Samuelsson giving press conference regarding the shooting of Suyana Sapaki.*]

Daniel couldn't afford to look worried and he'd forgotten what being casual looked like somehow, so he walked the length of the corridor without turning his head until he reached Suyana's room, and pushed open the door without knocking. Seemed like the kind of thing an IA type would do.

She was already sitting up, and he recognized her expression—the flash of ambivalence before she went in to romance the Americans, resigned but desperately thinking of a way out—before she saw him.

the publicity stunt of the year. Maybe she'd set it up herself and cut Samuelsson out of it. He was beginning to think she had it in her to arrange quite a bit.

Eventually, they watched as Samuelsson, unflappable behind the safety of the mic, issued her sentence.

"Due to the nature of her injuries, Ms. Sapaki's prognosis is, at the moment, unknown."

When Magnus glanced at the camera and down, Suyana sucked in a breath through her teeth. Daniel watched a dozen things flicker across her face and vanish.

Then she said, "I have to get out of here."

Daniel blinked. It sounded like Samuelsson was spinning his wheels, which was useless but seemed reasonable enough when you didn't want to admit you'd lost the person you were responsible for. What had she seen?

"I don't—"

But she'd already swung her legs over the side of the bed and was struggling out of her hospital gown.

"I know that look on Magnus. He's about to cut his losses. I have to go."

She didn't elaborate, but the hair stood up on Daniel's neck. He thought of Samuelsson saying, "Are you ready to be charming?" and the flicker of sympathy that had gone through him, even then, that this was the person Suyana was stuck with.

Before he could think better of it he said, "What do you need?"

She looked like she was debating sending him on another errand, like she knew this was her last chance to shake him before he got to be trouble. Not that he could convince her otherwise. He tried a smile. (Don't care, don't care.)

"Your name."

It felt like giving in, which was strange. "Daniel."

A moment later, she said, "And clothes."

He let out a breath that sounded more relieved than he'd meant it to. "Sure."

It wasn't difficult. The hall was nearly empty, and most of the patients unconscious. By the time he came back, she'd wrapped her IV puncture to keep it from bleeding—it matched the wide white bands on her left arm and her right calf—and had two rolls of gauze in hand.

Planning to be on the run for a while. He wondered where she thought she was going, with half of Paris out to find her for one reason or another.

She slid into the pants and shirt, and it wasn't until she was looking at the boots that he realized she must have been nearly naked before.

He said, "Here," dropped to his knee to help her into them, hoped she couldn't see him flushing. He wondered if snaps had an ethical line they shouldn't cross. If you drew the line at underwear, or if there were snaps just for lingerie shots. "Can you stand?"

There was pressure on his shoulder as she pushed off the bed, and her hand shook, but she said, strained, "I'll make it."

"Then let's go."

She pulled back. "No. I can go alone."

She couldn't disappear on him again. "Tonight I'm working on retainer," he said, just shy of flirting. "I'll show you right to your door. Whatever door."

She looked at him. Her eyes got hard at the edges sometimes. "Can we stop pretending that you're not working for someone?"

His face stung hot, like she'd slapped him.

"I'm grateful for the help," she said. Her voice sounded different; honesty, maybe. "But this isn't your problem, and it isn't your business. Don't get involved where you don't have to."

It was sound advice—from her face it seemed she meant it, and he knew she'd lost people—but it grated.

"I didn't just impersonate IA Ops for laughs, you know. I came to make sure you were all right after the gunfire I pulled you out of." He put some weight on the last words— he wasn't above guilting her.

"Get out while it's an option. Cut your losses."

She was right, if he were a normal person. But there was still a story here, and it wasn't as though she was rich in friends at the moment. She needed him. He could kill two birds with one stone; he'd keep his conscience out of it until later.

"Too late," he said, shrugging. It wasn't quite true, but it wasn't a whole lie. And he wasn't out to kill her, which was more than some could say. He just wanted to know how all this shook out. Any snap would.

She thought something over, frowned. "Onca?"

"Pardon?"

She shook her head, coughed. "Sorry. Sometimes when I'm tired, my first language—you know how it is."

He did. He'd been so exhausted a week ago that he'd fallen into Korean with the busboy at the hotel and gone a full sentence before he corrected.

"Who knows you're here?"

"Just the receptionist, who thinks I'm one of your handlers. Police are coming, though."

"You might regret the first one," she said, buttoning the last button on her too-big shirt. "I have to get to a restaurant. Café de Troyes."

"All right," he said. He knew better than to ask why. She wasn't in the habit of overinforming.

She looked much better for a couple of hours' rest and some painkillers, and she limped out of the room under her own power. He fell in behind her.

The buzzer sounded at the end of the hallway as the doors opened.

"Let's go," she said, glanced over her shoulder. (To see if he was there, he thought, and tried not to be pleasantly surprised.)

He started to make a joke—of course he was still here, who was he, Samuelsson?—but something about that wasn't very funny.

As they neared the doors, she said, "People might recognize me now that my picture's been on the news. I might need your coat."

"Forget it," he said. "You get one coat a night. That's it."

As they turned onto the street, he could have sworn that, just for a second, she'd smiled. It felt better than it should have; the pang of guilt felt worse.

6

Suyana's wallet and diplomatic ID were gone.

It was a problem—diplomatic IDs were valuable to the wrong people, and at the very least it left a trail at the hospital. But it was a worry for later. It went into a drawer in the cabinet Hakan made her imagine, where nothing touched. It was how you kept from going mad when your life was a series of careful lies.

Her first worry, her necessary worry, was how quickly she could get to Café de Troyes. Her second and third worries were what would happen when she got there, and what to do with Daniel.

But she figured anyone as adept at stealing as Daniel

would have cash, and when she said, "Cab?" he only said, "Unless you want to hug me all the way there," before he held out his arm for a taxi.

She bit back an answer, because there was no future in it. If he was half as clever as he thought he was, he'd abandon the gallantry before he had to start explaining himself, and she had a meeting to think about.

Diplomats couldn't afford to be careless. That was how countries crumbled. She'd come close enough to that before; she was in no hurry to repeat it. If anything went wrong for the UARC, she'd be the first one who disappeared.

Maybe Magnus already had a replacement waiting. Maybe when he had looked her up and down outside the hotel it had been circumspection, and a hope that the next girl would make a better first impression than Suyana did.

As the cab squeezed into traffic, she looked over and caught Daniel watching her. He must have been feeling guilty about something; his smile didn't hold.

Good. Let him worry about himself. She had a part to play. There would be another part to play if she got out of this in one piece and went home. There would be another after that, for the cameras, and one for the Americans to save face, and another and another and another, trading out of the vast catalog for the rest of her life, masks that never touched.

The first time Hakan had explained it to her she'd nearly

cried. But the longer you did it, the easier it was; you didn't feel like much of a person, after a while, but that was a problem for later too.

"Who are you working for?"

His face froze, and a passing streetlight illuminated him as he tried to decide which lie to tell her. After a moment he smiled, brief and thin. "Nobody yet."

It looked like the truth; that was a surprise.

"Am I worth more dead or alive?"

He sucked in a breath, said, "Alive," in a tone like she'd offended him by asking.

He had to be kidding. Whoever he was, he knew enough about the IA to guess how things turned out for Faces who were unlucky.

"You sure?" she pressed, voice low and measured, the voice she used when she was just short of a threat. Daniel had to lean in to hear her. "All of us have enemies. Somebody knows how much it's worth if my body shows up in a plausible accident."

He took that in for a second, gnawing on the inside of his cheek. "How many of them would try to shoot you?"

Armchair detective, too. Wonderful. Still, she fought back a smile. This felt almost like a real conversation. "That list is longer."

"I'll bet," he said, grinned. "But I'm not on it."

She parroted his smile. "Not yet."

He winced, laughed. Then he shook his head and sat back against the seat. "I remember that scandal. About Chordata trying to blow up the American post, and the guy who went missing and everything. I thought you were doing better these days."

The guy. Hakan. "The guy" was the highest-ranking diplomat the UARC had ever reached in the IA, and Daniel didn't know a goddamn thing.

But she had to focus. She forced tension off her face. "Hard to say. You don't really know until your TV minutes are high enough, or you're allowed to chair a committee, or you're seeing someone and they poll the other country to see how you're going over."

"Poor Ethan," Daniel said, with a smile that might even have been genuine.

That was a name she'd never mentioned; Daniel already knew who she'd been there to see.

Her fingertips were cold. She counted two breaths, in and out. (Figure out who he's working for. You know he's a thief. He's lying, he's looking for money, he's not out to kill you, he's still here. Who is he?)

He slid his hands in the pockets of his jeans—hiding something, such an obvious sign that she usually used it as a double blind. There was no way he was diplomatically trained. Wherever he was from, he'd never seen a day in the IA.

He said, "I'm beginning to get *very* curious about who you're meeting."

"I bet."

He pulled a face, and the flirty voice vanished when he said, "You were nicer when you were bleeding."

She couldn't help smiling. "I bet."

In the reflection from the window, he glanced out the opposite way, peevish. She wondered if this was how it usually was with people, where you could be exactly what you were feeling and not care.

"Faces aren't meant to be honest," she said. "Bad for morale."

He was reaching for his billfold, trying not to look at her and not doing a very good job. "So I was getting the act, before?"

The cab pulled over. She rested one hand on the door handle; then she glanced over at Daniel through her lashes, licked just the center of her lips the way Martine did when she was on TV and trying to win the boys over. He dropped his eyes to her mouth, back up.

"Daniel," she said, the lowest, sweetest voice she had. "You're still getting it."

She was on the pavement before he could pull his face together, and the cab actually moved forward (her stomach dropped) before it shuddered to a stop and he jumped out.

He looked like something from a movie—some careless glamour that struck her, all at once.

(Who would break you out of a hospital unless they had something to lose?)

"This way," she said, put the river at her back, and started walking.

Couples wove in and out on the narrow pavement, and she slid her hands into her pockets and limped beside Daniel, glancing at the faces that passed. Was one of them the person she was looking for? What if they hadn't heard the news, hadn't sent someone to the regroup point? What if they'd decided to get rid of her?

What about Daniel?

(Not your problem, she thought. He can deal with the consequences. That's a worry that doesn't touch your other worries.)

A familiar awning came into sight—the street felt strange in three dimensions, but there it was, just like the postcard. She felt a weight off her shoulders. Daniel was looking at it with all the disgust someone who stole designer peacoats could muster in the face of a tourist trap.

"Can we just go pick up a holographic Eiffel Tower for you to take home? There would be more dignity in it."

Touristy was the point. It took no notice of strangers.

"This is your last chance," she said, looked him in the eye.

"Keep walking, and you don't have to worry about any of this."

Please, she thought. Be smart enough to run.

He dragged his bottom lip through his teeth and looked at the restaurant sidelong.

"There's nothing in there for you. This is handling a hazard of the trade, that's all."

Something flickered over his face—fear, doubt.

"I'll watch your back on the way in," he said finally, straightened his shoulders, and glanced behind him.

She felt a pang, just for a second, looking at him. (If he meant that, if his lie was a small one, if she could trust him at all, that might be a fine thing.)

Then she moved past him and stepped inside Café de Troyes.

"At least we can eat," Daniel said behind her.

"You can. I'm vegetarian."

"Of course," he said, gave her a face.

But she hardly noticed. The riot of decor and voices faded as her focus narrowed to the small table in the back corner where a couple was sitting. The woman was facing the door; on her white sweater was a brooch shaped like a jaguar. And as soon as Suyana walked through the door, the woman was watching her.

Suyana's heart pounded, but she put on her best blank face, met the woman's eye only for a moment before she asked the host for a table.

He frowned at his bookings. "I'm sorry, but we have no tables, unless you'd care to wait?"

"No, thank you," she said. "We'll try again."

She turned to go a moment before Daniel could react, and she lifted her bad arm out of habit before she could remember.

Before the pain could really hit her he was holding the door; he followed her into the little courtyard beside the restaurant and hovered beside her when she sagged against a wall, safely out of sight of the street.

"I'm sorry," he started.

She shook her head. Sometimes she wished she smoked. Hakan had decreed that was something for later, when she'd aged out of being a Face and moved into handling. ("Too easy to give yourself away if you get nervous," he'd said. "Use them when you really know how to use them.")

She put her palms to the wall behind her back, where she couldn't fidget.

"Any plans to tell me what just happened?"

She looked up, said as discouragingly as she could, "No."

He shrugged, turned to face the far door of the courtyard. Whatever he was doing all this for, she hoped it was worth it.

She tried to guess how long she had to wait. Two minutes felt like ages when you were waiting for this, your legs shaking and no watch to go by.

"Someone's coming," Daniel said, a moment after she saw movement from the corner of her eye.

Her lungs went tight. "Stand back," she said, and to her surprise, he slid a few feet into the shadows without argument.

"Who *is* this?" he asked, voice tight and low. The last word shook.

She said, "Don't talk unless I talk to you."

It was the last thing she had time for before the woman reached them.

> [*ID 29907, Frame 104: Suyana Sapaki standing beside Daniel Park in courtyard beside Café de Troyes (no relevant street address). Unidentified woman entering frame, facing away from camera. Sapaki is looking toward unidentified woman; Park is looking at Sapaki.*]

Suyana's regular contact in Paris was code-named Zenaida. They met when Suyana was in session at the IA. Suyana would arrange a spa day (even Magnus was loath to follow), or vanish into Printemps; Zenaida would appear, and Suyana would try to ignore the thrill of being waited for. Zenaida was in her forties, shorter and slighter than Suyana, and it made sense they'd named her after the family of doves. She had a quickness and a kindness that made Suyana feel she would have confided in Zenaida even if she wasn't meant to.

They'd gone over what should happen if Suyana ever hit real trouble. Zenaida had never mentioned what happened after. Did they have to start over? Would she ever even see Zenaida again, now?

How many people would she have to lose, just to stay above water?

A shiver went through her; Daniel started to reach out. She ignored him, closed her eyes, imagined opening the drawer she needed, and let everything else fall away.

This woman was tall and slender, with light-brown skin and dark hair pulled back into a bun, and her black coat hung so long it made her look a little sepulchral. "I'm lost," she said.

"You should turn left at the river," Suyana said.

"But how do you know where I'm going?"

"There's only one rue Onca in Paris," Suyana said.

The woman nodded, and Suyana felt like someone had loosened a vise around her lungs.

"We've been waiting," Onca said. "Glad you made it."

Onca's face hardened as she looked at Daniel, and Suyana saw she was already thinking the worst, that any second Onca's unseen colleague would show up and make Daniel disappear.

Suyana had no strategy—she didn't even look over her shoulder, there was no time. She just held out her good arm toward him, palm facing him, as if warding off evil.

"He's with me," she said.

Then his hand slid into her hand. His skin was warm and dry, and there was the press of his palm, his fingers brushing her fingers; she tensed, and then he was slipping away and her hand was empty.

It was just enough to suggest something—to suggest anything the woman needed to see.

"I was told you would come alone," Onca said.

Suyana raised her eyebrows. "Circumstances changed. Help was necessary. You've seen the news."

She sighed. "You've been compromised. It's . . . worrying."

"So was getting shot," said Suyana.

Daniel smothered a nervous cough in his sleeve.

The woman looked at Suyana a moment longer. Then she smiled a little, said, "This way. There's a car near the bridge."

As they moved to follow, Daniel scanned the sidewalk in both directions, and walked close enough to Suyana that she felt as though he expected to prop her up. Under his breath, he asked, "So, how are things going?"

There were a couple of answers to that, but his presence had shifted the frame of everything (circumstances had changed), and the worst thing about politics was how often your worst-case scenarios were true.

"If anything happens," she said, "run for it."

He didn't say another word, and all the way across the

bridge, she carefully didn't look at him; she could practically hear him regretting it all.

The nondescript building had no elevator. Suyana leaned hard on the banister as they climbed, but she never once looked at Daniel for help. When she appeared at their door, she had to be standing under her own power. Still, he stayed beside her all the way up, hovering.

The place was a well-curtained nothing, with a little couch facing a few shabby armchairs and a television on an old coffee table. There were two desks against the walls, computer equipment and books piled high. Their cover must be students.

One man was at a computer. Another was sitting on the couch too casually, and she could only guess what weapon he was holding half-hidden behind his right leg. She hoped it was a knife. They frowned on guns, Zenaida said. But Suyana had never been in the field, and who knew how principles like that held up when you were in the mud.

She'd made some decisions today she never would have made in theory. Circumstances dictate, sometimes.

"Weren't expecting company," the man on the couch said.

Onca said, "Couldn't be helped. She couldn't get out alone."

"The stitches might have come out," Suyana said. "You have a medic?"

The man at the computer raised his hand without looking up.

The point man gestured at the TV. "They're talking about you. It's not good."

"Stories change," Suyana said. "When can I talk to Zenaida?"

"We're trying to determine if it's safe," said Onca. "You must be very tired. You should rest."

The last time Suyana had met Zenaida had been at the perfume section of Printemps, where Zenaida had made very knowledgeable faces at a shopgirl for fifteen minutes and talked about the drawbacks of osmanthus. She'd bought two bottles, and handed them to Suyana as soon as they'd left. "Don't have a sense of smell," she'd said, grinning, and Suyana had laughed and taken them and admired how well Zenaida could play her, that she enjoyed it.

Suyana filed it away as The Last Time I Ever Saw Zenaida. The words felt heavy, like she was going to tip over. But she was tired, that must be why; she had to take care of herself while she could.

"We'd love to sleep a while," she said. Daniel shifted his weight beside her. She added, "And eat. I'll get my stitches looked at after."

Onca nodded. "This is Ocyale"—the man at the computer raised his hand again—"and Nattereri." She tossed her coat on one of the chairs and crossed to the desk, leaning over Ocyale. Nattereri stood up and slid his knife into his belt.

Daniel didn't freeze up, which meant he'd seen it. Suyana was proud. She hoped it meant he'd last the night.

She was sometimes still a fool, and got friendly with the people she was using; they'd have no such problems taking care of any trouble.

"Tell your friend to take his hands out of his pockets before we pull them out," Nattereri said casually. "I'll see what there is in the kitchen."

Suyana glanced over her shoulder, where Daniel was standing with his hands at his sides, looking as if he'd been hit by a sack of bricks.

"Welcome to Chordata," she said.

7

It happens slowly, which they must have known to do. Things like that aren't accidental. When she thinks about it later, she gets a taste at the back of her throat like she put out a cigarette there.

They moved to Huánuco when Suyana was young; her memory of their first home was just the sun across the hill. Her mother sold trinkets to tourists. When Suyana wasn't in school she'd sit on the blanket beside her mother and watch the sea of faces and think things about them—their heights and their clothes, who was too loud and who was a thief—very carefully, long lists, in Spanish. (She shouldn't speak her mother's Quechua; school said so, her mother said so.)

x x x x x x

She started losing words, little sudden empty places, when she was nine or ten. It worried her, worried her more that she could remember them at home and lost them again on the walk to school.

Her mother shook her head when Suyana asked, and she knew better than to ask the teacher, but on the walk from the market she'd pass tourist kiosks and feel a fist in her stomach going tight. She remembers postcards of Machu Picchu now, green and deep blue and clouds like cigar smoke.

She's forgotten what the land-rights group was called in Quechua. Aqui, No Mas in Spanish. They told her later.

She's forgotten what made her mother go—if it was some great crisis or a series of little yeses. (They'd probably meant her to forget the reason; it's the kind of thing they want you to set aside.)

She marched alongside her mother, and her mother was smiling, and the fist in her stomach loosened every time they turned a corner and people were waiting to join them.

The police waited around a corner too. Her mother told her to run. It hadn't lasted long.

Hakan told her later he'd been informed there was a potential recruit in the cells, and Suyana figures she must have looked so angry some government toady thought she'd have the stamina for what was coming.

He wore a suit, and he was Quechua; the first thing he ever said to her was to ask if she was all right.

She knew when an adult was feigning kindness. In Spanish, she said, "What do you want?"

He smiled. He had laugh lines.

He made it sound exciting to be in the International Assembly; it sounded like she could be powerful (Suyana imagined bracing her hand palm-out, watching the police vanish). There was free school and new clothes and living like a movie star, and when she gave him a blank look he switched to talking about how she'd get to decide how her country was treated. He waited a long time to mention how it would be good for her mother not to work in the market, not to worry about jail again.

It was like instructions for taking a test in school; a lot of things that sounded helpful, about something you had no choice in. He sat very still. He wasn't nervous about what she would decide.

He had a pen in his handkerchief pocket. She thought what would happen if she reached for it, turned it so it stabbed him in the heart.

"You're a smart girl," he said finally, looking her in the eye, and it sounded at last like he was talking to her and not to a child. "This is a good offer."

It wasn't—you didn't have to talk so long about a good offer—but she wasn't going to get many others.

"All right," she said.

He smiled just at the edges of his mouth, said, "It's a pleasure to meet you," with a hanging pause at the end where her name would go. She counted to thirty before he grinned in earnest, held out a hand to help her up.

"I'm Hakan," he said, and his smile was full of little tests she already knew she'd be looking for, all the rest of her life.

Math and science and literature was the tutor.

How to handle ridiculous utensils and how to walk in high heels was the deportment teacher, who came so rarely Suyana could tell she was valuable, and paid attention so she wouldn't have to come back often. She brought a posture yoke with her, to teach Suyana how a diplomat looks. Every lesson she had her shoulders ached, the yoke straining around her as if she were a wild creature.

At home, she watched discs of other Faces being officially introduced and giving interviews after disasters and some clips of Faces on dates together who looked like they were being spied on, but was all stamped OFFICIAL in a lower corner by their national press.

Home was a studio apartment in Lima. When she looked outside, she could see the ocean. It was beautiful and spread out into nothing, and even though the waves came and went, the horizon never changed. She tried to remember when she picked up the wrong fork that the little waves were less important than the smooth emptiness you reached farther out.

Hakan taught her IA regulations and voting procedures and the history of the UARC.

"It's younger than you," she said with surprise when she looked at the dates, and he raised his eyebrows and said, "Perhaps not something you should say out loud," and she closed her lips around a test she'd failed.

The governments had decided to go ahead over the people. Now they were partners with Brazil, and neither of them particularly liked the other, so the only real comfort was how much they both distrusted outside miners and harvesters and how it was easier, now, to coordinate refusals and use local resources. (*Local* was the wrong word, she learned early; if too much money crossed the border that no one had really forgotten, then it was grumbling and protests on both sides.)

Still, it wasn't so bad, Suyana thought. You could probably manage if you just hated the same things for long enough.

"What about when I marched? Who was trying to take our land? The Americans?"

Hakan looked at her a moment. Then he told her about the cabinet he wanted her to imagine, in which she should put things that shouldn't touch anything else.

"Faces don't march unless their government would like them to," he said. "They have never marched against their government."

Now she knew. (She took note of the way Hakan had given her the truth.) And that meant he'd lied about where he found her; he must have lied about her to everyone. He was taking a risk with her. They shared a secret.

"It can't be just me for this job," she said. "Brazil must want somebody."

He smiled—the polite one, empty. "Brazil and Peru are united in their vision of a shared future. And the selection isn't for two years."

At night she sat in her room, practiced that smile in the mirror.

Soon school was in Portuguese.

Things she memorizes and puts away in a vast cabinet that casts shadows over her, things that can only be looked at one at a time:

All the countries in the IA. Their current Faces.

Extant relationships between Faces, possible relationships between Faces, relationships that had broken badly and were not to be spoken of, and the relative rate of return on the underlying diplomatic matter.

Who among the Faces are their allies. It's a short list. When she says, "Jesus, we're all alone out there, what's Carlos been doing at the Assembly?" Hakan gives her a look, says, "I wouldn't know, I requested a home assignment when I heard he'd been appointed Face," which tells her everything.

The fork on the far right of a place setting means to expect oysters. They'll already be shucked. If they aren't, look for a young man to shuck them for you. Shuck them yourself only if you're alone with a dignitary in front of whom you want to appear effortlessly competent. (Too bad; slipping the knife inside and cracking it open in a single motion was the only thing she could do right the first time.) Then the only problem was pretending you could stand oysters.

Everything in the newspapers. Thirty a day, maybe more: most from the UARC to determine how they felt about today's disasters, and then a few from the outside, to determine how everyone else thought the UARC should feel about today's disasters. (Thing she didn't learn until later: how rare it was to see the news without it being filtered through an attaché or a handler. Half the Faces she met were only meant to read what their handlers gave them. Hakan was putting faith in her.)

High heels are made to distract—distract the person wearing them, distract people who like them. When she stands on her balcony in them, it feels like she's going to tip into the sea.

Two years later, she got polished by a room full of dour women so she looked glamorous enough to deserve a dress she never chose, smiled into television cameras she'd never been told about, and said how honored she would be to become the UARC representative. She got interviewed in a parlor by someone who looked like he belonged to a committee—or six committees, judging by the pins on his lapel.

"What do you think of your opponent?"

She hadn't known she had one.

"I don't like to say *opponent*," she said. "We're all united in our dedication to the UARC. Whoever gets appointed will represent the confederation admirably."

He made a note (with pen and paper, how much more staged could this get?). "How do you feel about Hakan withholding from you that you have an opponent?"

That made more sense. She smiled, corners of the mouth stretched up in the way they'd taught her looked most natural on camera, and said, "I suspect a Face in the International Assembly knows that sometimes the people above you have their reasons."

There were fifteen more questions. None of them mattered; she'd answered the only two they'd wanted to ask her.

In the car she said, "They told me I had a rival."

Hakan looked at her in the way she thought might be unconscious, one frown line drawn between his brows as if willing her to understand him. "I know. I watched the interview."

"Do I have one?"

"No," he said, and she never knew if he meant there had been one, or if there wasn't one anymore.

They took her to Pucallpa for her official picture, because the UARC wanted to remind people of the resource they were protecting.

She'd never seen so much low land and water and bright, muggy green all in one place. It was too beautiful to be diplomatic about. As they flew over it she pressed her forehead to the window; as the stylists (a different team from the last team, more polished, she'd moved up in the world) tried to settle her in for the shoot, she was craning her neck to catch the black-headed herons, the jewel-toned flash of parrots. Shadows moved between the trees; she tried to keep her eyes open and her gaze focused long enough to get a good look at whatever was hiding.

The outfit they'd put her in was ridiculous—some faux-Incan beaded thing that might have been meant for her to look attractive, but took on water like a sack of rocks and snagged the dual braids they'd draped over her shoulders. ("Very cultural," one of the women said in Spanish with an accent Suyana didn't recognize.) The man who took her picture never wiped the look of disgust off his face.

Suyana gritted her teeth, counted her breaths, tried not to agree with him. She imagined holding out her hand and watching him vanish.

After the man handed his camera off and left, Hakan said something quiet to the assistant. She nodded and motioned Suyana a little forward, took a few photos. Suyana felt like her anger could crack her face in half, but Hakan's polite smile got a little bigger, and he wandered off.

"Beautiful forest," the assistant said.

Suyana took it as a cue to smile more. "Yes."

"First time seeing it?"

"Yes."

The assistant looked up from the camera. "I have someone who can take you inside, if you want. It's disappearing. The mines, the roads. You should see it while you can."

It was the first time in three years Suyana had heard "if you want" in a way that sounded like the other person wasn't sure of her answer.

"What's there to see?" she asked. A trap, she thought. It's a trap. Hakan.

But the assistant's eyes gleamed, and she said, "Everything."

Recruitment, Suyana realized. She was an official Face now; people would be trying to recruit her to their side if they thought she could do them any good. This might not be a cause that would live long. She didn't think she could do much good to anybody, but there was no knowing that until she tried to do anything at all.

She looked at the sharp line of the river against the tangle of the forest, felt like she was standing somewhere higher, somewhere dry where nothing touched her.

Here, she thought as if from far away; here and no farther. Suyana said, "Yes."

They made cards out of one of the shots she took. Suyana looked angry—too angry, said the state secretary who looked at it—but it showed up in *Profile* magazine and they called her "Sultry Suyana," and that must have been enough to please the Confederation. She didn't have to reshoot until the next year. That was in a studio. They'd put her into the same background, they said, so there was no need for her to go home.

The photographer shook her hand, told her it was an honor; he said, "I loved the exotic-sexy thing you were doing, let's see that again."

x x x x x x

As she stepped out of the water from the first picture she ever took, Hakan asked her a question in Quechua. She looked up at him and couldn't answer; she didn't know what he was saying.

That's how it happens. They fill you with the things they want from you, and you can't hold on.

8

Of the things Daniel had ever suspected Suyana Sapaki of being, while he made guesses about Magnus and her intelligence and her plans and her taste, being a mole for an ecoterrorist organization had not fucking been one.

He kept his hands open at his sides. The last thing he wanted was to give them an excuse to pat him down. The camera card was burning a hole in his pocket.

"You all right?" Suyana asked.

It could have been gloating—maybe it would be, later—but right now she had a stone face on, and her mouth was tight, and he knew the real question was: Are you going to betray me and do something stupid?

She'd given him fair warning. In some distant part of his mind, he rewound to the door of Café de Troyes and wished her good luck and walked across the bridge and into the night. Maybe he stole another camera and set his sights on a Face who was less trouble. Why hadn't he done that?

Because this story could change countries. Because it would be the making of him.

Because in the hospital she'd looked at him and, just for a second, had been happier to see him than anyone had ever been.

"Mostly," he said.

She looked at him a moment longer, and he could see her doubts multiplying.

Then the woman (he'd forgotten her code name, he needed to pull himself together and start playing this game) was showing them to a bedroom with one bed, and a sturdy desk piled high with paper and pens and glossy magazines. It had a distinctly penitential feeling, and only Suyana's calm kept him from panicking when the woman closed the door behind them. He held his breath, listened for anything that sounded like a bolt sliding shut.

"We're not prisoners," Suyana said. "This door only locks from the inside."

He wasn't sure which was less comforting: that she'd read his mind, or that she'd been looking for locks.

She sat heavily on the bed, leaned her good shoulder on

the wall, breathed out as she closed her eyes. It was deep and low, and more than just a respite from running with wounds. It was the sound of someone resting for the first time in a long time. What was your life like, when your work as a terrorist spy was the most comfortable you got?

"So," he said, then didn't know how you brought up the topic. He settled on, "Friends of yours?"

She smiled, just at the edges. "Not these three. I meet a friend, sometimes. These are strangers I'm supposed to go to in an emergency."

Well. That explained the knife. He sat beside her, his hand an inch short of touching her hand, and looked at the space between their fingers. She was too pale, still.

"We should have stolen you a pint of blood from the hospital."

"Good idea."

There was a moment's quiet. She opened one eye and looked him over, like she was a dragon and he was doomed. "Why did you come back there to get me?"

There were plenty of flippant answers, but he couldn't really think of any. The back of his neck was hot. "It seemed wrong to leave you there," he said, shrugged. "I didn't think you'd want to live through a shooting just to get poisoned in a hospital." (Anyone who reacted like that to her handler's face was well aware of how short life could be.)

She licked her lips, like she was preparing for an even worse question, but she must have thought better of it. She was looking at the ceiling now, breathing like she was fighting sleep. She said, as if she was asking herself, "Where did you even come from?"

Seoul, he almost told her. Seoul, where I abandoned my career, where I took the right picture at the wrong time and had to run. She'd understand.

"The alley across from the hotel," he said, tried not to feel like a coward.

She didn't even open her eyes. He hoped the Chordata people left them alone long enough that Suyana could rest.

He looked at the door. "How bad into this are you?"

She thought a moment. Settled on "It's been a long time."

He didn't know what to say. He'd never guessed. She'd shown some initiative here and there, but not enough to make her a subject of interest; in all his research there had never been a breath of anything suspicious. Good for her.

She turned to face him, winced as her leg shifted. Her stolen boots were too small in the calf—he'd had to pull out four eyelets and tie them lower—and he wondered if they hurt.

She watched him. "Hakan warned me people would try to recruit me for everything. Mining partnerships, bases for military operations on our borders." She frowned, glanced at her foot and then out at the far wall. "He found me after a protest, so maybe we both should have known, but I don't think it ever occurred to him someone would try to recruit me for something I wanted."

He recognized what was happening. She was so tired she was telling him things she shouldn't; she was telling him the truth because there was a good chance he wouldn't live long enough to tell on her.

He should have been terrified. He was—he liked to think he was reckless, but there was reckless and there was being held at knifepoint. Mostly, though, he looked at her bloodless face and her trembling hands and the eyelids she couldn't keep open, and was sorry for her. He wanted to lock them in until she'd really rested. Everything else could wait.

He cleared his throat. He must be getting tired too, if he was going soft. "How long?"

"A Face five years. Chordata the same."

Shit. "So you knew them when they blew up the American outpost three years back."

Suyana looked at him and raised one eyebrow, just an inch. It felt like someone had doused him in water.

Of course she knew them then. She'd told them.

She didn't say anything, but she looked lonelier than he'd thought possible, and hopeless.

I can't tell, he thought, sudden and heavy. I can't tell anyone. She'd lost her handler to that fallout. She'd nearly been deposed. Her country had almost been ruined. All to save some forest for a little while from a country that didn't know how to take no for an answer. What a thing, when you're nineteen—how do you carry something like that and keep going?

She'd dozed off—or passed out—and for a few minutes he sat in the quiet, listening to her breathing and the sound of his heartbeat in his ears.

Maybe she'd lost blood. He could call the medic.

But he didn't call out, and he never moved. She could use a little quiet with someone who didn't want to kill her.

Then she started awake, looked around with that hesitation you get when you're always waking up in strange places. He knew that feeling. His gut twisted.

"How old were you at the protest?"

"Almost thirteen," she said.

He thought about that for a second.

"I was sixteen when I saw you on TV," he said. "The welcome for new Faces. You were in a beaded dress."

She rolled her eyes, inched up a little from the bed. The distraction had galvanized her. "The IA stylists have shoved me into more beaded dresses and shawls than should ever exist. I never got higher than a C-minus red carpet grade."

He smiled. "Ouch."

"The PR materials always say it's highlighting our national

identity," she said. "Like there's only one. Like anyone's interested in helping us protect it. It can be pretty funny, so long as you don't think about it, but once you're in the chair it's not funny anymore. Some countries get their own stylists, but if you're using the IA stable, they don't much care who they're working for, and you end up looking the way they assume everyone assumes you look."

He'd rewatched that ceremony when he was reading up on Faces the first time. He was looking for Hae Soo-jin, but he remembered Suyana. She walked like someone had warned her she'd teeter and she'd been determined to prove them wrong, heels banging against the stage until she was in the center.

Then she'd stood, in her ugly beaded gown with impressionist rainforest designs across the skirt, and said in a clear, low voice, "I, Suyana Sapaki, vow to represent the United Amazonian Rainforest Confederation to my utmost, to protect and preserve it, and to aid the International Assembly in the creation of a greater and a finer world." You could see how much she meant it—too much for the pageant she was in. (He wondered what he had been doing three years before that, when she was getting arrested.)

"You looked like you were too good for the room," he said, without meaning to.

Her face was frozen for a second, recalibrating, trying to decide what his angle was. She was wide-awake, now, taking stock. There were shadows hanging under her eyes. He wondered if she'd ever been rested since the first time the IA got its claws in her.

He said, carefully, "Was that with your first handler?"

She nodded. "Hakan," she said, her voice thick. She cleared her throat. "Magnus came after. An IA committee appointed him; I don't know if they talked to the UARC government first or just decided."

Shit. Here we go, he thought. Draw her out. Get the scoop on Magnus. Build a story you can tell. (Some of this he'd never tell, because it was hers and he couldn't bring himself to, but he had to walk away with something, didn't he? Why had he protected her otherwise?)

He said, "There's a good sign."

She made an exaggerated face. "Magnus is a good diplomat—he gets things done, he's fixed a lot of messes—but sometimes when you're a good diplomat . . ." She shrugged her good shoulder to show what she thought about the trustworthiness of statesmen.

"He looks sharp on TV," Daniel said.

"That's half the reason he does so well."

It was a professional assessment. No lingering feelings that could be mined for a relationship story. Interesting. "So how did the Chordata people first reach you?"

She looked up sharply. Something in it must have

sounded too much like a reporter, or too eager—her expression was the face she'd given Magnus, not looking at him so much as watching him.

He felt, weirdly, like he was slipping away from something important.

Then there was a knock at the door, and the guy with the knife (Nattereri, he remembered) came in, holding a pizza box and water bottles.

"Don't suppose you have a nice red wine somewhere," Daniel tried.

Nattereri didn't even spare him a glance as he set it all down and looked at Suyana, slouched against the wall.

"Do you need the medic?"

"No, thank you. I'll get him to check on me soon." She frowned. "Is everything all right?"

Nattereri looked over at Daniel, which meant bad news that shouldn't be shared with strangers. Daniel bristled—who'd gotten her out of gunfire and broken her out of the hospital?—but maybe it was the sort of moral high ground he should avoid.

"Eat first," Nattereri said. "There's time later."

"There's time now."

Daniel didn't know how she could say that. He was so hungry the smell of pizza was making him dizzy, and without meaning to, he said, "You sure?"

Her eyes slid to him without her head moving.

"Give us ten minutes," she said to Nattereri.

When the door was closed again, she sat up and looked at Daniel full-on. "You might not want to question me again while we're here."

It felt like she'd just advanced on him. He squared his shoulders. "Is that an order?"

She slid off the bed far enough to reach the pizza and put it on the bed between them. "When you know the stakes, you can give the orders."

He thought about what she'd been through. He thought how odd and awful it was, that this was advice from experience. Whatever bad news was coming over the transom, he didn't want to ask what she suspected. (He worried he'd even survive long enough to find out.)

Instead he said, "All right," and handed her the first slice.

They ate in silence, their eyes on the door, Daniel's mind working in tight circles about whatever would be coming down on them next.

Two slices later, she said, "I'm ready," like she was talking to herself. As she stood, she reached for her hair with both hands—flinched, hissed.

Oh shit, he thought, her arm.

He reached for her braid. "I can help."

"I have it," she said through gritted teeth.

After a second, he dropped his hands.

She twisted it into a black rope one-handed and coiled it into a loose knot at her neck. Apparently she wanted to look elegant before the worst happened. Diplomat habits.

Daniel stood and brushed pizza crumbs off his coat. He debated taking it off—he'd look more as if he belonged—but there was something to be said for being ready to bolt if things turned sour.

Before he could make up his mind, she was pulling the door open and walking out as smoothly as she could for someone with only one good leg.

After a moment's hesitation, he followed. This was a story, and he couldn't let second-guessing get in his way.

(He thought how perfect her profile would look just like this, determined and grim, on the front page of the paper, and wished for his camera before he could help himself.)

Nattereri had taken up a new post. He was sitting in the hall, facing the door, his knife drawn.

Suyana was already standing beside one of the computer desks with Onca, looking over Ocyale the medic's shoulder at his screen—audio editing, it looked like.

Onca said, "It's Magnus. He gave another press conference about an hour after you left the hospital."

x x x x x x x

Daniel calculated—by then they had been in the courtyard at Troyes, or headed here. How much time had been spent looking for them, and how much of it had just been Magnus in his office in front of a piece of paper, wondering how to explain that his Face had vanished?

Ocyale pulled up a video window with a stuttering picture and a tinny version of a voice Daniel was already getting tired of hearing.

"—and I regret to report that, at this time, it appears that the United Amazonian Rainforest Confederation Representative Face Suyana Sapaki has been abducted. She was last seen being taken from a medical facility, presumably under duress. At this time, the affiliation and identity of her captors remain unknown."

Daniel tried to breathe, couldn't.

Magnus looked into the camera now: official, soulful. "It is with a heavy heart that, as a member of the UARC diplomatic team acting under protocol of the International Assembly regarding potential terrorist activity, I must officially sever all diplomatic ties with Suyana Sapaki."

Ocyale stopped the video. For a second the room was so quiet that Daniel could hear his heartbeat in his ears.

Burned. The fucking International Assembly had publicly burned her.

The last time the IA had tried something like this, maybe a decade ago, the Face had actually been abducted—the kidnapping was on closed-circuit footage they looped on TV for days. He'd shown up later holding a newspaper, in a hostage video full of demands.

Daniel realized he couldn't remember what had happened to that Face. That wasn't comforting.

He glanced over his shoulder at the door, where Nattereri looked like he was wishing for a gun.

Then Suyana said, "But that's not everything."

"No," said Ocyale, sounding surprised she'd guessed. Strange that he hadn't given her much credit. Daniel already knew better.

"Here. This went out on a secure channel, about the same time as the press conference."

A stranger's voice came over the line. "To all field agents: Suyana Sapaki upgraded to alpha priority. Expend all necessary effort to locate. Do not engage under any circumstances. Report directly to Douglas and await further instruction."

"I don't know a Douglas," Suyana said immediately, never taking her eyes off the computer.

Onca closed her lips around the question.

The Shadow Assembly Comes for the Queen of the Amazon, the headline would read. Daniel saw it rolling out on every channel. Maybe it would keep her safe, he thought. Publicity would make her harder to disappear.

He liked that. It made him feel a little less queasy about

having pizza with someone whose cover he'd been trying to blow.

After a little quiet, Onca cleared her throat. "We understand this is no fault of yours, but the situation has changed."

Suyana ran her teeth across her bottom lip, a flash of white no one but Daniel could see. "I would hope," she said, as if from far away, "that Chordata realized something like this was always possible, as I did—this could happen under any number of circumstances unrelated to any discovery of my involvement."

It sounded like she was disappointed in a family. Maybe she was.

"Of course," said Ocyale, more sympathetically than Daniel would have expected.

What was their arrangement, exactly? What was Suyana to Chordata? Informant? Lieutenant? You didn't do all this for some everyday mole. She had an investment here.

How much of this did Magnus know?

"But things are dangerous," Onca said. "It's not just that they've cut you. They're still looking for you. What if they find you?"

"Find us" hung unsaid.

Suyana closed her eyes a beat too long, like she was looking out for a far-off ship and had gotten tired. "Give me a minute. I need to decide what to do. Please don't trouble yourselves in the meantime; I won't ask for your support until I'm sure I'll need it."

There was just enough condemnation in the words that Daniel flinched.

Nattereri asked, "And your friend?"

Daniel held his breath.

"He's with me," she said.

His chest went tight for a second. He tried not to let it mean anything. Didn't work.

He didn't dare speak—she'd been clear—but she had to know he'd offer his help the minute she asked. His stomach was going sour. Help was still help even if he wanted something from it; she still needed him; it wasn't as though she was thick on friends.

"Wait for me," she said to him as she passed him. "I won't be long."

It was her diplomatic voice, smooth and distant and impenetrable, trying to stave off the worst.

As he closed the bedroom door, she was standing in the galley kitchen across the way, silhouetted in the yellow light from the street below, looking like a tower of ash left behind from where disaster had struck.

She deserves better, he thought suddenly, fiercely. Better than me, better than all of this.

Then his phone buzzed.

9

Suyana leaned against the kitchen counter, propped on her arms (ignored the throb of the wound), gripped it until the edges stung her palms.

It was stuffy—she needed fresh air, she needed to *breathe*—but she fought the urge to go to the window. No use in getting spotted like that after all this trouble. She'd be back in the line of fire soon enough.

The street was silent. She felt so lonely her eyelids ached.

The information fanned out in front of her, a fractal of choice. The biggest threat was Chordata's potential unwillingness to shelter her if her information had dried up and she was nothing but a target. Those branches were short, and their ends blunt. It made her so angry she had to take a breath because her lungs were going tight. Hadn't she been everything they'd asked? Hadn't they acted like a family?

But her loyalties weren't anyone else's loyalties. She had to remember that or this was all over. She brushed those options aside. It would do no good to press them from a place of no advantage; she'd have to think of some other card to play.

But trees could overwhelm if you tried to see through them too much. There was what the Americans would do to the UARC if it was shaken and vulnerable. There was the stranger in her room now, who had helped her and was lying to her. There was the question of whose words Magnus was reading on television; there were questions about the subterranean search team that may or may not be his.

There was the question of the shooting.

It seemed almost nostalgic, given what had happened since. When she thought about the moments before the first shot, standing in the shadows of a contract while Magnus looked her over as though she'd been born to worry him, the moment had the sepia quiet of an old photograph.

Had it been Magnus?

Below her, someone on the street was calling out—a woman answered, laughing, and two sets of footsteps moved under the kitchen window and into the night.

No, Suyana thought. She could picture Magnus writing

the message that had gone out on the underground line—lightly, so there would be no traces on the blotter. He wouldn't have trusted a verbal message. Some things were too important. She could picture Magnus meeting Margot and the IA Central Committee, and calmly accepting their ruling that she had to be cut loose. She could even, if she was being honest, imagine Magnus suggesting to Margot that trying to retrieve Suyana would be effort for nothing, and it would be easier if she just disappeared. Magnus knew how to stay a step ahead of complications.

She could not, as much as she tried, imagine Magnus meeting someone in an alley, handing them her headshot, and saying, "We'll be there at half past two. Make sure you don't shoot me once you open fire."

She was almost sure he had grabbed her elbow just after the first shot, before she fell, as if to pull her out of the way.

(If he'd grabbed her elbow before the shot because he'd known it was coming, then she'd have a word with him after this was over.)

There were quieter ways to get rid of her. They could have sent her on a home tour, paid out her contract, and brought in the next Face in line. They could even have brought her home and killed her there; Faces were forcibly retired sometimes, when they'd outlived their usefulness, and nothing came of it. A Face dying on home soil was nobody else's business.

Magnus wouldn't turn her into a martyr bleeding out on the streets of Paris. That was just bad marketing. He was quieter than that, and he picked only the best for the job. If he'd set it up, she'd already be dead.

It was more surprising that she'd been publicly declared kidnapped. That angle showed somebody desperate to close the deal. The Chordata agents had no way of knowing how strange it was, but IA internal protocol assumed three days' leeway before kidnapping was officially considered. Sometimes Faces got tired of the game and dropped off the map; it happened often enough that they gave you seventy-two hours to wear yourself out and come home again.

Someone in the IA stood to benefit from discrediting the UARC, then, in case she should suddenly appear and make any damning statements.

She tried to forget about the Chordata strangers in the living room, about Daniel in the bedroom. She opened drawers in the cabinet where nothing touched.

Face relationships were kept under wraps until papers were signed, in case negotiations broke down. The only people from the IA who'd even known about her meeting with Ethan were the IA Ethics Committee that had looked over the contract, Magnus, and Ethan's team.

Chordata could have wanted to kill her, if they thought

she'd been compromised. They'd want her to take her secrets to the grave.

But Chordata was a secret that mattered; a secret she'd kept even from Hakan.

He might have guessed, once, the morning three years ago when he woke her to tell her Chordata had struck the American mining outpost and there was nothing left.

When she asked, "Was anyone hurt?" he gave her an odd look before he said, "The buildings were empty, don't worry."

After that it was a scramble to look decent before Margot arrived with the Central Committee's comments, and Hakan watched her tying back her ponytail, took breath for half a dozen sentences he never uttered.

(If he'd ever guessed, it must have been just at that moment; he had the face of a man who had underestimated someone he loved.)

The Committee's comments were specific. Margot delivered them herself.

"You must condemn this action," Margot said, her face expressionless, her voice like a radio spot. "Terrorist activity will not be tolerated in the IA. It's bad enough that this has happened at such a delicate time for the UARC's reputation—Hakan, we'll discuss this later. There will have to be an immediate response. We've scheduled a press conference for you in an hour—we'll send a stylist up."

"Thank you," said Hakan, at the same time Suyana said, "No."

She'd been so terrified that it was hardly a word, more a desperate breath she pressed her lips around, but it sounded like a shot in the little sitting room, and when Margot turned to look at her Suyana felt like she'd fired a weapon.

"I beg your pardon?"

But Suyana couldn't take it back. There was only forward, into an anger that was becoming an obstacle, but she wouldn't condemn them. She wouldn't.

"If this is a delicate time for our reputation, going on television for such a small thing will only make us look more troubled." It occurred to her only after she'd spoken that it was what Margot had intended. She set her teeth.

Margot narrowed her eyes. "Small thing?"

"It was property damage. No one was hurt. Why would I go on television to condemn vandalism?"

"Because these are terrorists," Margot said, utterly reasonable. "They're out to harm your country."

"Oh, that's different," said Suyana. "But the list is incomplete. Four years ago the Americans came over to revitalize Altamina silver mine. When they left, they buried two tons of waste. When my government complained it was leaking into the groundwater, they covered it with sand. That's harmed more lives than this explosion. I'm happy to go on TV and talk about threats to my country, if you insist, but if I do, I want to be thorough."

She could hardly breathe as she said it; her bravery was drying up.

For an awful second, nobody moved, as if she'd been so angry she'd managed to stop time.

Then Margot turned to Hakan. "And this is how you've trained the Face of the United Amazonian Rainforest Con—federation?"

Hakan looked at Suyana with an expression she didn't understand, and said, "I train diplomats, not puppets. She must know her own mind."

"I see that," said Margot, raising an eyebrow. After a moment longer of looking at Suyana, waiting for a change of heart, she stood. "Well, we certainly wouldn't drag her to the podium against her will, and there's no need to make this a laundry list of complaints. We'll issue a general statement denouncing terrorism. I assume you stand with us?"

"Of course," said Hakan.

When they were alone, Suyana said, "I'm sorry." She felt like she'd been punched in the stomach. Her hands were trembling.

Hakan shook his head. "You're a better diplomat than that."

"Margot was trying to lower us. No matter what I did it would have been wrong."

"You can find ways out of that, Suyana."

"I got angry."

"The UARC isn't in a position to be angry. Too much still relies on the Big Nine. Chordata are terrorists."

"They're not," she said. "Not like Margot says. You know they're not."

"They're not helping you," he said.

It was the closest he got to telling her, if he knew.

"Margot isn't helping us," she said, but the venom was already gone. She was looking down the limbs of a tree that had nothing but Margot at the end of every branch.

After a moment he said, "Not anymore."

He left after that, to talk to Bolivia about some chance at positive PR that could help drown out the noise this would make for them.

The IA's official denunciation of terrorism in the heart of a troubled, unstable UARC ran without them, on every channel.

Three weeks later, Hakan was gone.

Suyana had gotten better at seeming docile since.

One of the things that kept her up at night was wondering if she would ever have told him, or if she would have kept it secret, something that was hers.

She'd told no one else about Chordata, until tonight. Then she'd shown it to a stranger, a stranger under her protection, because he was the reason she was still breathing.

She was in a bad way now, having let him help her, having walked across Paris in the shelter of his arm, having fallen asleep in front of him, an unforgivable weakness. No good would come of Daniel. But if it came to that and the IA swallowed her up as punishment, only she and Daniel were at stake.

No, she thought suddenly, with a rush of fear so tense that her arms spasmed.

Kipa knew.

Kipa, Face of New Zealand, was young and unassuming and knew more than she let on. Chordata had already made contact, to see if she might be an asset.

(Suyana wasn't supposed to know that—recruitment wasn't her brief, and Chordata liked to keep the left hand ignorant of the right hand—but Zenaida had confided.)

If the IA had tried to kill Suyana because they'd found out about Chordata, then Kipa was in danger too. She'd have to be warned. The IA had a clear path to Kipa if they wanted to remove her. She was so young still, and even more alone than Suyana.

The warning would have to be in person; Kipa wouldn't believe the news from anyone else's mouth. She was smarter than she looked.

If you were going to work with Chordata, you had to be.

x x x x x x x

Chordata wasn't a terrorist organization—not like some. They hit empty buildings; they sabotaged equipment; they were careful not to take a human toll.

But Chordata had grown, and they were more fractious now than when they'd first taken her aside. They might not risk a loose end if they thought she'd been compromised. They couldn't afford to. She understood.

(She got so tired sometimes from looking at things from every angle, as if her eyes would split.)

That meant she wasn't safe here. She was persona non grata with the IA, too, unless she showed up at their doorstep with an airtight story.

It would have to leave out both Chordata and the Americans, explain how she had been targeted but had escaped alive, and catch Magnus where he was vulnerable—his reputation. It would have to leave out Daniel.

Her arm stung where the wound had started to tear. She folded her hand against it.

Daniel shouldn't be here. It was her fault; because it was easy to use people when you were desperate, and because, once or twice, it had felt less like recruiting a civilian and more like having a friend. What happened to him now depended on how she could use him best.

"Onca," she called. "If you have a moment."

At the door, Nattereri startled, tightened his hand around his knife.

Onca came into the kitchen on stockinged feet. She'd removed the leopard pin, and she seemed wary, as if she'd been called in for a fight.

Suyana wished that Zenaida had met her instead. Suyana wished that she had armed herself before she'd called on Onca.

(No; Hakan would have called it a weakness, to draw a weapon first.)

Suyana decided to skip the diplomatic runarounds. This wasn't the IA floor. "What's your rank?"

"Lieutenant."

Not bad, for a member who was barely thirty. Most people Suyana knew of who ranked that high in the emergency operations of Chordata were Hakan's age.

"How many are you in charge of?"

She looked uncomfortable at the question; Suyana guessed Chordata wasn't supposed to betray its full methods, not even to her.

"Ten in Paris," Onca said finally, "a dozen others in the countryside."

That was a fair number, and far-flung. Panthera Onca had been embraced into the inner workings, then; no way to know how far up, but Suyana was relieved to be dealing with someone who'd made tough decisions.

"Have you ever killed anyone for Chordata?"

It felt like longer than it was before Onca said, "Yes. Once."

"Why?"

"Self-defense," Onca said, shifting her weight as if to better defend her position. (Did Suyana look like she was in any shape to attack?) "It had to be done."

Suyana had known a long time that the sunny dreams that recruit you are the lip of a long, slippery stair into what they really wanted from you. Chordata had asked her to kill, once; mostly, she suspected, just to see what she would say. From the safety of the perfume department, she'd refused. She could guess the situation Onca had run into, where someone was lying and word had to be stopped before it spread. That was always a danger; it was why she'd never breathed a word to Hakan.

She didn't want to make any other guesses about what Onca might have done, when Chordata asked her to.

Suyana said, "What do you know about me?"

"That I'm to preserve you."

But that was just parroting the order Onca had been given; in between Onca's breath and her words, there was a glance away that betrayed her.

Suyana tilted her head a little forward. "And what do you suspect about me?"

Onca looked at her sidelong. "That you're Lachesis."

Suyana knew the name. She'd used it a hundred times; she'd *chosen* it. Still, something about the way Onca said it made the hair on Suyana's neck stand up.

(Lachesis were the pit vipers. They had no rattles in their tails, so you didn't even know you were near one until it had its teeth in you. Zenaida had said, "That's why I chose you as my asset. A sense of humor."

Zenaida hadn't smiled. Suyana hadn't either.)

Suyana kept her face blank. "What makes you think I'm Lachesis? You must meet with assets all the time, if you're doing emergency work. I could be anyone."

In the streetlights Onca's skin was bronze, and her eyes were wide and bottle-green. "No. Once I saw you, I never doubted it was you."

"Why?"

Onca smiled. "Because you were shot, and you still made your target just to tell us what you knew."

Suyana blinked twice, tried to breathe.

She could not fail.

Chordata existed in a dozen countries with no real leader to collect them, just groups of believers borrowing the network: organized units or loose affiliations or a handful of people guarding what was left of nature, whatever it meant.

To the IA, Chordata was a cell of anarchists near the rainforest that occasionally took UARC matters into their own hands. It was unimaginable to the IA that this wide a network even existed. To them, any serious revolution would want to announce itself as a worthy combatant. A group like Chordata worked smaller, most of the time; it was easy to miss. The irrigation projects in Turkey were held up by faulty equipment until the legal appeal stopped the digging, but that could happen to any project that big; phone-cam footage of illegal waste dumping in Canada went viral online, but any shithead teenager with a phone could manage that. It was a series of unfortunate coincidences that robbed corporations of their peace of mind, but so far, there was no pattern most people could see. (Suyana wondered sometimes about Margot; Margot hadn't gotten to where she was by being slow to see patterns in a possibility.)

Chordata would be hunted down by every soldier the IA could spare if they realized what they were up against. If Suyana were revealed as the spy under whom they flourished, the IA would get a witch hunt on top of it.

"Why were you chosen to meet me if things went wrong?"

"I had some trouble when I was younger," Onca said, a hint of pride. "I've worked with partners, but often I was alone in dangerous places. I carry that with me."

There was more to be gained with Onca by leveling, then.

"I'm in a dangerous place," Suyana said.

Onca nodded. "Do you know who shot you?"

"Do you?"

She blinked, recoiled an inch. "No."

"I had to ask," said Suyana. "I'd understand, if Chordata had heard something about me being outed and loose ends had to be cut."

Onca was quiet for a second. "You'll have to keep thinking, then," she said, prim. "We don't set up emergency protocols for people we're trying to kill."

"I'm sure, but I'll admit I was hoping. It would be easier to discuss things with you. Everyone else on my list will be a lot less happy to see me alive, and a lot less likely to listen."

Onca seemed to sympathize with that. She thought it over a moment, sighed.

Suyana was so weary she could barely stand. She looked at the kitchen floor, a maze of tile underfoot, and tried to narrow things down, to put aside whatever couldn't be helped and hold to the bottom line.

She'd been cut loose from the IA by its most powerful committee. Magnus had let her hang.

She gripped her arm until it stung.

She had someone gunning for her on secure channels. She had a young man in the next room who knew more than he should, whose motives she didn't know. And if she was going to make it out of this, she had to lever her way back into the public eye, some way that the IA couldn't dismiss.

Finally, Onca said, "What will you need?"

Suyana looked up.

"A corpse."

10

When Suyana opened the door, Daniel stood up from the bed and tried to look calm.

Her expression was half-ravaged, half-absent, and for a second he felt a little sick, wondering what decisions she'd been making. That wasn't the face of someone who had chosen the easy out.

"You look like you have some marching orders," he ventured.

There was a flicker of something he didn't understand, something pulling tight. She said, "My wounds are clean. They're getting me some clothes. Then we have to go."

"I'm up for it," Daniel said.

He smiled, made fists inside his coat pockets until his nails cut into his palms.

He'd answered the phone, which was his first mistake. He'd bought it with a disposable number in anticipation of the bidding on Suyana's photos, but hadn't used it yet. He knew better than to answer a phone whose number he'd never given anyone. He was losing his grip.

He gave a deep, clipped "Yes," like he'd been waiting to be placated by some underling and was about to start knocking heads.

The voice on the other end said, "Daniel Park."

He nearly dropped the phone. There was no way to know that—he'd paid for everything in cash, he hadn't given his real name since leaving home.

He held on with both hands, feeling like an amateur. The edge of the phone pressed uncomfortably against his temple.

"Nope, sorry. You have the wrong number. Who is this?"

"It's come to my attention," said the woman, as if he hadn't spoken, "that earlier today you took unauthorized photographs of an IA Face with the intent to profit."

This was it. This was the IA security team, and they were only calling him so they could pinpoint where he was before they stormed the place.

"I have no idea what you're talking about."

"That's unlikely," the woman said, "since I'm looking at a camera we recovered that has your fingerprints all over it."

Breathe, Daniel thought. (He thought, They really don't waste time before they put the pressure on, do they?)

"Did you get it from the bastard who stole it from me?" he snapped. "What an asshole."

The woman laughed—round and genuine, and for a long time. When she finished he had the phone pressed to his ear so hard his earlobe ached.

"I'm not government. And I'm not interested in the camera. I want to talk to you about what's missing."

The data card burned in his pocket. Hang up, he thought. Then: this is the call I've been waiting for.

"Okay," he said. "Talk."

Once Suyana closed the door, her shoulders sagged; still more poised than normal people, but she looked a little less like she was addressing the nation. She let out a breath just short of a sigh, pushed her fingers into a steeple, and winced down at her wounded arm as if she'd forgotten about it.

Her fingers must ache, Daniel thought; she must be as tense as he was.

He fought his first instinct, which was to push past her and make a run for it.

His second instinct—to reach for her shoulder—was

stranger, and somehow more dangerous, and he sat back down on the bed and pressed his curled hands into the bedspread just so he wouldn't be tempted.

"You look awful," he said.

She shot him a look, raised an eyebrow.

He bit down on a smile, moved aside. "Lie down for a minute, if you want. You could use the rest."

"You're starting to sound like Magnus," she said, but still she lay down, trying to favor both her left arm and her right leg. She wasn't tall; it was easy to forget, but she fit on the bed with her head well short of the pillow. Magnus always towered over her in pictures.

"Given how today has gone, I take offense to you thinking I'm like him," Daniel said.

Her eyes were closed, but she rolled her head toward him. "He does what it takes."

"And what about when he sold you out just now?"

She went still for a moment, and he felt guilty when she opened her eyes. That much more rest, gone.

"It solved his problem. Looking for me would be embarrassing, and cutting me off put the UARC in a position of sympathy and public support. He's not a good person, but you don't have to be, to have your reasons."

She sounded very understanding for someone who had nearly died. She must be really tired.

That necklace was still in his pocket. It felt heavy, unwieldy, like it knew they were talking around it. He opened his mouth to ask, *Are you forgiving him?* but the words didn't make it.

Suyana's eyes were closed and her hands slack, one along the bed and one across her stomach. If she kept pushing herself on no rest, she'd die from flesh wounds, which wasn't as heroically as she'd probably want to go.

He frowned at the necklace he'd spread across his palms, tried to see if he could remember which stone had been turned over. (It bothered him a little that Magnus had found fault, that he'd turned one of the stones in his fingers like it was an extension of him and not her.) Then he shoved the necklace and card into his pocket and licked his teeth, thinking what the look on Magnus's slick diplomat face would be when this story broke.

It was good. It kept him from thinking about what the look on Suyana's face would be.

Things someone can know, before they ever call you on a number that you never gave:

- how you were in the alley of a hotel at five minutes to noon with a stolen camera and no official IA itineraries; how you'd come from Korea alone, with only cash in your pockets, and how it must be so different from home (a city that was never mentioned, but *home* was spoken with grave import, and Daniel thought about the picture he'd taken and the family he'd abandoned and could hardly breathe);

- how you impersonated an IA operative to break Suyana Sapaki out of medical care;

- how you met up with notable people and walked through the city, through a tourist crowd that should have lost any trails, to a flat that had a pedigree with certain types of people that the government did not look upon with fondness;

- that they can tell you all this without caring what it reveals about them, because they have so much more where this came from that it was just politeness on their side not to put the bullet in your head first and then read you the evidence;

- how to make you realize, before they ever level with you, that you were going to do whatever they told you to do.

There was a knock on the door an hour later; it had felt like longer, like night would be over before anyone came to find them.

Daniel started and dropped the magazine he was reading (the annual International Assembly Gala feature—Suyana wore a gown patterned with huge palm leaves, rated C+).

"I have her things," Onca said when Daniel answered.

"But she's sleeping." He frowned; what on earth did he sound like?

From behind him, Suyana said, "I'm ready."

When he looked over, she was already sitting at the edge of the bed, smoothing her hair with her good hand. She sounded younger when she was tired. It was awful, somehow.

Daniel stepped aside to let Onca in, feeling like a bouncer, and moved for the hallway so Suyana could change.

Nattereri looked him over as he passed.

"I'm not changing," Daniel said. "I look fine."

Nattereri flexed his knife hand, the fingers spreading out over the blade and back around the handle. "How'd you say you ran into her?"

"Blind date."

Nattereri raised his eyebrows, shifted toward the edge of his chair, and rested his forearms on his knees.

Daniel winked at him, leaned against the wall, and wished the bedroom door would open again already.

When Onca finally came out (sparing Daniel one circumspect look he didn't like), he slid in without waiting for an invitation. Too late, he hoped she was fully dressed. He closed his eyes and put up an open hand. "Sorry for the bad manners, but if I stand in the hallway any longer he'll stab me."

"Serves you right," Suyana said, and then, "Everything's decent."

After all that subterfuge, he'd expected her to come out looking like an IA charity gala, long gown and gloves and swinging earrings. He'd have wanted to see that.

Instead, she was barefaced, wearing her stolen boots and black pants and a black button-down, and had a square black scarf in her hand, and it was all so plain he thought she might as well have stayed stolen.

"Please tell me I don't have to wear this too."

Suyana shot him a look. "It's what I asked for." Then she turned to Onca in the doorway. "If we don't make contact in three hours, close the route."

Onca nodded, her face grim, and vanished.

Daniel turned to Suyana. "Where did you tell her we were going?"

"To try to make contact with Magnus off the grid, and see what the word is within the IA about my shooting, and what can be done."

He had an unsettling moment, a quiet click in the back of his mind as he heard the words hidden under the words.

"Where are we really going?"

She looked startled. After a moment, she grinned.

"I'm sorry," Daniel said. "I can't help you. I didn't get anything good. You hear gunshots from somewhere, you get the fuck out of there, you know?"

"And where are you now, having gotten the fuck out?"

Damn, that voice would pry off your fingernails without you ever noticing.

"Nowhere."

"Mr. Park, you're not the best liar we've come across. Here or on your forged papers."

She was not doing a good job convincing him she wasn't government. She was, however, doing a bang-up job of painting Daniel into a nasty corner.

His uncle had forged his papers. If she followed that trail with any intent, it wouldn't go well back home. She had to know that's what he was thinking, and which way he'd fall.

"Then why don't you just quit the show and tell me how you think this goes."

"I'd appreciate that," she said, sounding as if a veil had fallen away. He imagined her sitting back in her chair. "I'm better at the practical than at games."

I'll bet, Daniel thought.

He'd lost feeling in his wrists and ankles. As she explained, he sank slowly onto the bed, as if his body, inch by inch, was giving out.

As he and Suyana left the apartment building, he fought not to look back at the flat, fought not to look around at whoever might be taking pictures of them.

(Daniel could usually spot a camera at twenty paces—how could he have missed whoever this woman had slipped into the crowd?)

"We'll split up a block away from here," she said. Her limp was a little better; she kept too far away to lean on him. "I have to go on no matter what happens, but turn back if you need to."

"You keep trying to make me turn back," he said, glancing over. "Isn't it too late? Either you trust me or you don't."

Her hands disappeared inside the pockets of her shapeless, borrowed jacket.

"Yes," she said, not looking at him. "I guess it is."

She knew how to discomfit him with the minimum effort, he'd give her that. Maybe that was his own fault, asking for a straight answer when he wasn't sure he'd recognize the truth if she told him.

Still, his heart had twisted, just for a second, in between "yes" and everything else.

They came to the corner, where the narrow street opened onto the avenue.

"We should stay out of sight," he said. "Keep to the small streets. Some of your friends might have followed us." He looked behind them.

She shrugged with her good arm. "Until they can prove I'm a loose end, it's better for them to leave me alone than kill me."

God, how did you walk without looking behind you when that's what you were up against?

"Fine. Then I just hope they're loyal enough not to kill us before we get there."

"Me too." She turned onto the avenue. "Let's go."

They crossed in the middle of a crush of tourists and ducked off the avenue again a few streets later, where they could connect through back streets for a while without hitting the security cameras of a hotel.

Daniel didn't look behind them. Whoever might be following would just have to get in line to murder them. (The hair on his neck stood up, thinking about it.)

"I don't understand the hold they have over you," he said finally. "They're ecoterrorists who nearly ruined your country's standing in the IA with a single stroke. Is it just a message? Is it the forest? It doesn't make sense to me."

She looked up sharply. It must have sounded strange.

For five streets they were quiet. Then she said, "It would, if you'd ever seen home."

It was his turn to glance over. She looked tense and wistful, like she was thinking of a country she'd never set foot in again.

His lungs ached. He wrapped his fingers around the card in his pocket. He opened his mouth to tell her the truth.

"We're here," she said.

× × × × × × ×

"We know where you are," the woman said. "We'll have someone make contact with you once you're on the move, at a
point where you can provide us with the card as a gesture of
good faith. If we like what you provide us, we'll make an offer
of employment."

"What if I can't provide?"

"That's probably not in either of our best interests."

He didn't doubt that for a second.

(On the other side of the door, Suyana was talking with
Onca in a low voice; decisions were being made.)

"All right," he said, his stomach churning. "I'll keep my
eyes open for any of Ethan's business that seems interesting."

The woman said, "We're after Sapaki."

His mouth went dry. He hung up.

Suyana opened the door.

11

The IA annual portrait had to be taken in the Palais Garnier, because nothing else would hold them all, but at the request of several national press outlets, for the most recent portrait a few weeks back they'd been arranged in rows in the orchestra section instead of on bleachers on the stage. It made for a more regal picture.

"Thank God," Ethan had said to Satoshi as they settled in. He'd forgotten to undo the button on his blazer, and it was straining across his shoulders. "Those bleachers reminded me of high school."

"You've never seen a high school," Martine said from the row behind him. "Stop pretending to be populist."

Suyana was seated a few rows behind them, between the Netherlands and India—strategically less desirable than among the Big Nine, but from here she could watch the whole expanse of formal suits and carefully selected cocktail dresses, which was always illuminating. The IA floor was regimented; it was different, watching Iceland's and Turkey's Faces chatting from adjacent seats as their handlers stood helpless along the far aisles, clenching their fists at the possibility of untoward statecraft they couldn't wade in to prevent. Stylists moved quickly through the rows, silhouetted like puppeteers as they arranged the last of everyone's hair.

"I've seen the inside of a lot of high schools, Martine."

"Movies don't count," said Grace from beside Martine. Down the row, China and Italy laughed. So did Ethan.

"I mean I go on a lot of school visits," he said. "School visits count!"

"And so populist," said Suyana.

Ethan and Grace both turned to look at her; Ethan with raised eyebrows and the ghost of a smile, and Grace with an expression Suyana couldn't determine before she turned away.

"Okay, places!" someone called. On stage, three dozen photographers took up positions behind their cameras; the stylists melted away.

Suyana took off the leaf-printed jacket she'd been given.

The shirt underneath was plain and black. From the sidelines, Magnus started to say something, and settled for looking strained. When Suyana sat back in her seat, she saw that Margot had come onstage and was watching her, unblinking.

"Members of the International Assembly," she said, and everybody in the room fell silent. Ethan, midjoke with Grace, froze, still twisted around in his seat, as if afraid to interrupt her by turning to face front.

"Thank you for being here today, and congratulations on another productive year. For those who have been here before, welcome back. Your exemplary work has been much appreciated."

Down toward the front of the orchestra, Korea's Hae Soo-jin shifted in her seat. Margot never looked down, but one corner of her mouth turned up.

Martine and Grace exchanged a glance. Suyana wondered what Hae Soo-jin had done.

Still twisted to face them, Ethan mouthed, "What happened?" Suyana couldn't hear Grace's response, but Ethan made a pained, sympathetic face.

Suyana thought about the contract Ethan needed to sign; the contract Magnus said didn't have enough appeal.

"For those who are taking their first portrait, it's a pleasure to have you in the Assembly. Let's all work toward a better world again this year." Margot stepped off the stage even before the applause could really get going. Suyana appreciated that. Margot was a monster for power, but at least she didn't bother grubbing for approval.

"All right, let's rehearse," the stage manager called, and clapped her hands. Before he turned around, Ethan gave Suyana another look, a longer look.

She pulled out her tablet and made an adjustment to her calendar. Global news updates would have to wait.

She was going to a party.

Magnus had written her three messages telling her to put the jacket back on. The last one just said, "National identity, please," and Suyana had to fight not to make a face. She kept the jacket off.

It was spring, and everyone was trying not to look intimidating; the Netherlands, India, and most of the rest of the row were in pastels. When the picture came out, Suyana was a negative space—black hair, black shirt—that tugged the eye.

"That was lucky," said Magnus when he saw it, with a sidelong look at her, which was as close as he got to praising her.

"Margot thought so too," Suyana said, which was as close as she got to confiding in him.

Terrain's facade was flush with the unbroken off-white line of buildings in its narrow street; the green door was so dark it was almost black. If you passed it, you'd think it was an old townhouse, and not wonder for a second about what was going on inside.

That was because places like Terrain could afford not to advertise.

"You're heading for the seventh door on the left," she told Daniel.

Daniel followed her gaze. "Looks deserted."

"That's the idea." She took the scarf from her neck and let it fall open at her waist.

When she tried to wrap the ends behind her back, there was a jolt of pain up her arm. She hissed and froze—she couldn't afford to make anything worse, she'd be bleeding all over the kitchen.

Then Daniel was behind her, his fingers nudging hers out of the way (they were cold).

"What's the idea here?" he asked quietly.

"Apron."

The fabric pulled tight around her waist as he knotted it; his knuckles brushed her back. When she looked at him over her shoulder (she didn't know what she was looking for), he didn't quite meet her eye.

"I'm going through the kitchen. Nobody pays attention to barbacks." She hoped. "You get to lie your way in from the front."

"Wonderful." He straightened his shoulders, ran his

tongue over his teeth. "How private is it? Just Faces? Members only?"

"Not quite, but the people who go there don't want to draw attention."

"Damn, and I was going to pass myself off as a gossip columnist."

"Don't joke. They caught a snap in there, once—he left on a stretcher."

For a second he went totally still. "More fool him, then."

"Well, he tried to get secrets out of Martine. You don't get much more foolish than that."

He pulled an agreeable face. He had a very agreeable face, when he wanted to. Then he sobered. "What happens if I don't get in?"

"Wait for me here. I'll meet you as soon as I can."

She hoped he was smart enough not to stick around. Tonight wasn't going to get any easier.

He did Suyana the courtesy of pretending he hadn't already come to the same conclusion, but when he spoke his voice was a little tight. "What if I do get in?"

"Then I owe you a drink."

He looked at her, on the verge of saying something. Then he closed his mouth, shook his head. "Good luck."

She saluted him with two fingers at her temple as she turned and headed for the alley.

It was a quick stop at the corner tabac to pick up some milk and then hobble as fast as she could to the kitchen door of Terrain, head down and looking harried, one of the dozens of brown people who worked there and were so interchangeable to the people in charge that they hadn't bothered to replace the dead batteries in the security cameras.

She'd noticed that the first time she'd ever been here, more than two years ago. By then, she was good at looking for a quick escape.

As soon as she was in the kitchen, someone snatched the bottle out of her hands. She kept her head down, waited for someone to blow her cover.

"Get up there with the food!" he snapped in Spanish. "Table five!"

Well, that worked, she thought, picking up the tray.

Still. She'd been here three weeks ago as a guest at the portrait afterparty. There was some small pang, thinking how hard she worked to make the UARC respectable in the IA, how many times someone had braided beads and feathers into her hair when the cameras would be on, how easy it was to become invisible as soon as some assumptions were made.

But now wasn't the time to look a gift horse in the mouth. Her anger would hold.

She grabbed the tray and balanced it on her shoulder

with her good hand. She could manage—she'd gone through three years of deportment in the posture yoke. She could balance a tray up a flight of stairs.

The music was vibrating through the soles of her boots when she was halfway up. By the time she reached the back bar, it was shaking her to the teeth. It had to be her nerves. The music hadn't seemed this loud the last time she'd come here. She was trembling and hot with terror; her bun was searing on the back of her neck.

Terrain's designers had tried to strike a balance between the sleek modernity that made people feel like the booze was worth the journey, and the colonial-era nostalgia that made people feel smug about having the chance to pay through the nose for it: dark wood floors, leather sofas, curtains in deep-green velvet, and sharp-angled chandeliers suspended above the dance floor out of reach. (No one swung from the chandeliers at Terrain. There were other clubs in Paris if you wanted to be tacky.)

Just past the curtains where Suyana stood was the long tortoiseshell bar that curved the length of one wall, and then the dance floor with tables studding the edge, and at the far side of the room, one step up from the crowd, the faux-antique booths and low sectionals where Faces held court when they came calling.

As soon as she set the tray down, a waiter scooped it up

from the other side, handed her his empty one, and headed back out. Suyana wiped it down just to look busy, and peered across the dance floor.

Come on, Kipa, she thought, do me a favor and don't be dancing.

Kipa was young, and quiet by nature (unfortunate for a Face, but New Zealand must have their reasons). It meant she was just as likely to be dragged reluctantly onto the dance floor as to demur. If she was dancing in a clump of Faces, this was going to be a disaster.

Suyana didn't tend to call attention like some—when Martine or Grace took the dance floor, a circle opened up around them—but once you were declared kidnapped and your embassy cut you loose on the evening news, you probably got famous fast.

Half the reason she'd sent Daniel to the front was in the hope he'd cause a scene and draw attention. She couldn't afford to be noticed before she found Kipa.

But there she was, slouched in a banquette in the abandoned Faces mezzanine. Relief flooded Suyana; Kipa having been disappeared would be too much to take.

Kipa was a slight, wiry figure, and even with her face obscured by her dark hair Suyana knew she was torn, trying to decide if it was worth braving the dance floor.

That was how Suyana had found her to be about most

things: always on the verge but undecided. She'd recommended against Kipa when Zenaida brought her up.

("We're not supposed to pollute the waters," she'd said, "but I was curious what you thought about a Passerine in the fold."

Passerines—the order of songbirds, thousands and thousands of species. Chordata used Passerine for most of its low-level informants; they sweetly sang to their contacts whatever it was they knew, and no one ever suspected. They differentiated after that, in ways Suyana wasn't told; she wondered which genus Kipa would be known by. What did you call a bird that wouldn't survive the winter?

"If you're asking me, you already know what I think," Suyana had said, flinching away from a perfume that smelled like flowers two weeks decayed. Zenaida *hmmm*ed and reached for a bottle of Hierophant, shaped like a throne and costing more than Suyana made in a week; it smelled like marble floors and the mint that grew in the mountains back home, and Suyana excused herself before she was tempted to buy it.

What Zenaida had really been telling her, Suyana realized now: *Look out for her.*)

Suyana and Kipa were friendly, as much as you could be in the IA, and Kipa was the right sort of person for diplomacy based on kindness, but Chordata was dangerous work, and they'd found her too soon.

Chordata hadn't listened. Kipa had campaigned in New Zealand for marine preserves, and supported a bill that gave tax breaks to solar and wind power. It was a gesture of good faith as far as Chordata was concerned—if she'd campaign at home, she'd campaign in chambers—and they needed everyone they could find.

But Suyana knew what was working against someone trying to keep their head above water in the IA. Kipa's predecessor, Alex, had campaigned for Maori reparations, to the point of starting a petition among Faces to make an amendment to the IA Declaration recognizing any indigenous population that wanted to sue their government.

Suyana hadn't joined. Hakan had given it his blessing—some Quechua pride might up her approval numbers at home. But Suyana knew what Hakan didn't, and she couldn't risk being on anyone's radar. Moles kept their heads down.

It came to nothing. As Suyana guessed, calls to action weren't what the IA was looking to hear from its Faces, and when Alex tried to bring the motion to vote, the cameras were turned off, the session postponed, and Margot and the Committee visited New Zealand's handler.

Alex's mistake was the reason Kipa had been called up in the first place. She was too young by two or three years, but she was sweet, and her handler played up the idea she was preternaturally good-hearted. An editorial of her on the beach in a tutu, tee, and sneakers had sold a hundred thousand copies of *Atalanta* magazine last year.

Chordata didn't understand that Kipa would be useful only so long as she kept quiet about things the IA would rather not discuss. As soon as she spoke up, her clock would be ticking.

"Hey!" a bartender hissed beside her. "What is this? You on break?"

He sounded like he was winding up for a long go at the help. She slung the tray on her good shoulder, snapped in Spanish, "I'm going, I'm going!" and slid around the bar and out into the crowded club.

She scanned the dance floor as she walked. It was old habit to pick out Grace dancing alone where no strangers could reach her, Natalia and Satoshi parked near the bar, and Martine, holding her electronic cigarette out of the fray as she danced smack in the center of the crowd. (Ethan wasn't here. Very respectful of him.)

They all looked occupied—not even Martine seemed bored yet. There was time to reach Kipa and warn her, if she'd listen.

At the booth, she tried to set the tray down, but her arm shook and her wounded one was too slow to catch it, and amid the clatter and bang she took out two martini glasses. Shit, shit, too much attention.

"You all right?" Kipa asked. She was already looking past Suyana, reaching across the booth for napkins to mop up the spill. She was too nice for the IA.

"Had a twinge in my arm," Suyana said.

Kipa froze. Slowly, she turned and registered Suyana; the color drained from her cheeks.

"Get that look off your face," said Suyana, still kneeling, trying to look busy. "And keep your voice down."

"But—" Kipa cleared her throat, tried to look casual. "You were shot. Kidnapped, they said. They think you're dead." She sucked in a breath. "Magnus already burned you."

"I heard."

"I don't know anything," Kipa said. "I'm sorry."

Suyana frowned. "Why would you know?"

"Why else would you have come?"

Fair question, given how Faces were trained to look out for themselves, but still Suyana's heart sank. She shook her head. "Kipa, I've been with friends, and news is pretty bad. I came here to warn you. Until I know who shot me, you need to be careful."

Kipa's face fell in. "Someone's after—your friends?"

Suyana looked Kipa in the eye. "There's a chance whoever shot me *is* our friends."

As that sank in, Kipa's eyes got painfully wide, tears pooling at the corners. But after a few seconds she frowned and blinked and nodded, steeling herself, and looked fixedly out over the dance floor with her chin high. "Okay. Okay. All right. What about you?"

Control and compassion. It was encouraging. Kipa was young, but she'd been in the IA a year—the first year was always hardest—and Suyana hoped she'd come out the other side formidable.

"I'll handle myself," Suyana said. "When you go back, get one of the plainclothes for your hall. Call your handler in as often as you can, never leave your apartment alone. Give me a word."

Kipa frowned. "What?"

One song was winding into another. They'd be back from dancing any moment.

"A password, Kipa." She could hear how frustrated she sounded. "So whoever I send can prove they're with me. You can't trust anyone until this is over. Don't use one you've given out already."

Kipa stammered, "Violet."

"All right." The new song was grating, the drums a panicked heartbeat she was trying to ignore. She'd been here too long.

She glanced at Kipa as she piled the last of the mess on the tray. "Go home with the others. Don't be alone. Don't talk to anyone who doesn't give the word. Don't tell our friends I came to see you—they don't know, and it might be dangerous for you. I'll send word if I can."

Kipa went green. "I don't like the sound of that."

"Imagine being me." Suyana half smiled, knelt to ease the tray back onto her shoulder. Her bad arm was throbbing. When she got somewhere safe, she'd have to look at the wounds. There was no way the hospital stitches would hold. "Be careful. Good luck."

As she stood, there came the tiny thunderclaps of two pairs of heels, and in her periphery, Grace and Martine flashed by in bright spots—Martine white and blue, Grace brown and silver.

Fuck. If they recognized her, she was doomed. They'd rat her out in a second to their handlers or the police, and she'd be disappeared as soon as Magnus could call up someone to finish the job.

Please, she thought, please never have looked me in the eye. Martine might not have. Martine never looked at anyone if she could help it. But Grace had seen her, she'd spoken to Grace, Grace would know who she was.

She held her breath, kept her head down and her shoulders hunched under the tray as she turned to leave. Grace was still moving through the exit path; there was a glimmer of purple that Suyana could tell was pretty pricey jewelry for an incognito night out.

(Daniel still had a necklace in his pocket worth a hundred grand. If the bouncers searched him and realized who'd borrowed it, he'd be going to jail for kidnapping.

She'd wanted him to be a distraction. She didn't want him gone.

Her hands started to shake.)

Suyana kept her head down, slid one step while trying not to crack Grace in the skull with the tray.

Behind her, Martine's electronic cigarette flared with a prerecorded crackle.

"Looks like you've been barbacking, Kipa," Martine said, voice like glass. "You should be dancing. There's a new taxi dancer, if you're not too chicken. Not quite handsome, but I'd love to know where he stole his coat."

Daniel. Suyana didn't even have to look up.

I'll be damned, she thought. He came in after me. She ignored the flicker of warmth at the back of her neck. This was their last stop; she couldn't bring him any farther. She took another step, another. She was past Grace—she was free.

"We won't make you," Martine was saying. "Real friends don't. I hope you didn't let the Amazonian put you up to anything."

Suyana froze. She had to move, she had to make a run for it, they'd raise the alarm any second—but though her heart was in her throat, dread held her fast.

She'd seen it before, when Martine got her hooks in and pulled; the panic on someone's face when they realized their number had been called at last.

Grace turned in slow motion, her attention torn between Kipa (eyes like saucers) and Martine, but still she put out an arm to prevent Suyana from bolting.

Suyana turned her head, gazed sidelong through the veil of glassware. Martine's face was in shadow, but her smile was sharp and ruthless in the false cinders of her smoke, and when she spoke, the little glow-light hardly moved.

"Evening, Suyana."

12

How to get into a club so exclusive it doesn't have a sign: walk in without looking left or right, stop in front of the bouncers, let out the sigh of the infinitely patient. Say, "My friend didn't tell me what ID you want, since she didn't know. You've never asked her for any."

When they ask, "What's your friend's name?" picture Martine Hargaad walking past them for years, let the image sink in so they can see you thinking about it.

Say, "She told me you'd know better than to ask."

When the first bouncer says, "I don't suppose this friend could ID you from your picture," say, "Given what I'm here for, I doubt she'd ID me to my face."

Slide your hands in your pockets. Shrug like a guy who makes his living taxi dancing on the verge of another long night, a guy who doesn't care what hidden camera's taking his picture.

"You're kidding," one of them will say.

Show them a tangle of platinum and gems. (Think about Suyana giving it to you, about your fingertips on her warm neck.)

Say, "I'm supposed to return this to her. She's pissed she forgot it."

Give them just long enough to realize it's genuine; slide it back in your pocket, out of sight of the cameras. Say, more earnestly than you mean to, "I don't think she needs it to turn heads, but I guess other people do."

(Remember you're supposed to mean Martine Hargaad, not Suyana. Refocus. Prepare to talk as long as it takes.)

Watch without saying anything as the bouncers start to make up their minds.

[ID 40291, Frame 86: Daniel Park entering Terrain,
carrying no visible cargo. Access ploy unknown.]

When Daniel was twenty, he applied for an apprenticeship with the Korean International Diplomatic Press Corps.

He got the job. A few months later, Hae Soo-jin's handler,

Madam Kim Hyun Jae, noticed him in the press pit, and invited him to join the team that shot the official candids of Soo-jin's private life.

He must have been an idiot, he thinks, when he can bring himself to think about it.

It took him two days to realize nothing about Hae Soo-jin was candid. She was never alone. Even her pajamas were selected by her stylist.

He took a thousand pictures of her having cell phone calls with no one on the other line, for use whenever news broke: smiling, frowning, tears that stood in her eyes but never fell. He took pictures of her with Murat Eren, the Turkish Face, whom she was dating on a short-term contract for some electronics-industry exchange that escaped him. They walked in and out of a movie theater arm in arm as he took pictures from behind a bush, so the blurry leaves in the foreground would make it look more spur of the moment.

He couldn't shake the feeling that maybe nothing about Soo-jin was candid because there wasn't much to her. She didn't have much to say to Murat that wasn't small talk, and being around her for any length of time was like mainlining a TV drama where no one deviates from the sheet in the writers' office. A hologram, he thought sometimes, when he was being mean, or when he felt sorry for her.

It was numbing work, and paid almost nothing, and he spent most of his time being lied to about what she was actually doing and coming home to a studio apartment so small he could touch both walls if he lay down and stretched his arms over his head. After a year, something about the combination of bad pay and bad information started to grate.

He'd only ever gotten one really candid shot of her, ducking into a coffee shop and chatting with an older man in line. There wasn't much to go on, but something about her (serious, suddenly, in a way she never was when she knew the lens was on her) sparked him to take the picture.

He used his phone for the next picture, and got a face ID on the guy. He was Global Trade Organization; they weren't supposed to be meeting Faces without official documentation and supervision.

There was only one snap agency he knew, thanks to a guy in the photo pit at one of the IA photo-calls. It took ten minutes to track down the phone number (their cover was a greengrocer) and tell them what he had to sell.

It took less than twenty minutes for Madam Kim to call him into her office and tell him that, as it was technically Korean state equipment, his camera sent her a copy of every picture he took.

"What did you think of that?" she said, eyebrows up, as if they were chatting over tea. "That was some catch."

And he'd been young and stupid and couldn't hold on to a lie any better than "I don't know what you mean."

Her face got more menacing by degrees as she spoke. These things were routine, she said. Hae Soo-jin was merely being polite to an official she happened to run into. Nothing was discussed.

(His official camera had a microphone. Soo-jin had talked about what it would take to decrease mandatory import percentages on rice, in the hope of bolstering domestic distribution. It hadn't been bribery, but they were getting there. It was the most he'd ever seen her care about anything. It was a story.)

"Nothing must happen to Hae Soo-jin's reputation," Madam Kim said, with a smile that came a second too late.

Daniel had been with this team long enough to know what happened to people who got that smile. "Of course," he said. "We all want the best for her."

There hadn't been time to copy the high-quality picture onto a disk, but Madam Kim probably would have seen that if he'd tried it; he sold the photo on his phone for cash, to a woman in a yellow raincoat who was waiting outside the DVD bang the man on the phone had named. It was enough money to run with.

Daniel picked up false papers from his uncle and was in the air by nightfall.

If he spent half the flight with a sour stomach, worried about what would happen to Soo-jin and trying to talk himself out of it, that was a first-timer problem. This was why nation affiliation killed journalism, he reminded himself a hundred times; once people were your friends you couldn't do what had to be done.

The IA hadn't sent her home, but she'd been taken off two committees and was on a six-month relationship freeze that the magazines trumpeted with the finality of death. He hadn't even been able to determine if Soo-jin made it to this session, or if she was just a ghost, waiting out a ticking clock back home.

He'd made a good escape, though. Clean. No one from home had followed him. He had a new camera, new target, new prospects, no attachments. He could recover from a shock. His life was a straight line.

That was before Suyana.

Inside, the nightclub looked like every dream of new money and every discretion of old money. The thing now, at clubs back home, was to have high ceilings and black marble floors and acrylic furniture. One of them (too scandalous for Hae Soo-jin) had art projected live on the walls by artists who you could instruct to make anything you wanted, usually tacky, often disturbing. He'd gone twice, but since he didn't have enough cash to make an artist draw something that would get gasps, there wasn't much appeal.

This place didn't encourage participation of any kind, and it fascinated him.

He moved toward the dance floor, one eye out for Suyana. The aesthetic from home was elite and knew it; this was more pristinely ramshackle, more insidiously snotty. He wanted, just for a second, to propose to the designer.

"You must be new."

The snap contact had found him. He froze.

Somehow he'd imagined the strike would come outside the club, if he was unlucky enough to be on the street alone; somehow he'd figured that by getting inside he'd outsmarted them. He was an idiot. Shit. Shit. He steeled himself and turned.

It was Martine Hargaad. He was so startled that he jumped, felt like an asshole.

She was just as pale as she looked on TV, more so without the warming amber lights the IA used for broadcasts; with her blue dress and blue eyes and hair so blond it was nearly white, she looked like a glacier.

He knew she'd been a Face for a long time—she had to be twenty-seven, maybe older—but up close he could see why Norway had never replaced her. Where would they find a better face than hers?

She was holding a cigarette, low at her side and untouched. All right, he thought. Careful. Don't fuck this up. (Don't be memorable, he thought, quick on its heels.)

He smiled. "Need a light?"

She made a face, held up the cig, and rolled it for a moment between two fingertips. It beeped and flared to life.

He remembered those, now that he saw one—pricey, but Faces were too important to risk lung cancer, something like that. Whatever you told the public to justify some people getting electronic cigarettes and everyone else getting ads for smokes that killed them.

"Just as well," he said. "I'm out of matches."

She half smiled, took a drag. Water vapor curled out her nose and left the scent of cardamom. "Haven't seen you here before. Tourist or taxi dancer?"

There was no right answer, the way she asked it. "Whichever one gets me a dance."

She looked unconcerned and horribly suspicious. He had no doubt, now that it had occurred to him, that a snap was watching him as they spoke. And somewhere in the crowd, Suyana was looking for whomever she'd come here to find, and trying not to be made.

"Taxi dancer," she said. "First night?"

From her tone, untested taxi dancers' corpses weren't worth soiling your shoes on.

"Oh no. Some women can handle a man who's more direct, that's all."

Her eyebrows moved even higher.

Daniel wished he could risk breaking eye contact to scan the place, but Martine conversed like she delivered addresses on TV, dismissive but demanding your full attention, and he didn't dare get distracted.

She was a black-and-white movie of some ancient queen who'd been famous for her cruelty. In other circumstances, he'd have liked it.

At last, she said, "Does that line ever work?"

"Not on direct women," he admitted.

That got him the shadow of a smile. (He was auditioning for a movie where she had a script and he didn't. This is what her kind were trained to do. No wonder Faces all lost their minds.)

She plucked her cigarette from her lips. "Let me guess," she said, tapping it as if it could ash. "You like them blond."

He shrugged. "Depends. If they have faces like yours, I could learn to like it."

She shot him a look. "I'm rich, too," she said, an edge sliding in. "I bet you like them rich."

That was a trap if he'd ever heard one. He wondered if the bouncers knew how Martine felt about taxi dancers, and let him in just so she could tear him to shreds. Too late now. Caught was caught.

He grinned. "Rich doesn't hurt."

"Doesn't hurt me," she agreed. The cigarette hovered against her mouth as she took a drag, the end glowing red like it was burning. "You could stand to be more subtle."

"No time. It's a long night if you're lonely."

"Yikes." She looked out across the crowd, said absently, "You could stand to be a *lot* more subtle."

"You could stand to cut to the chase a little." It came out sharper than he meant, he didn't know why. Had she seen Suyana? Was that who she was really looking for?

Her grin turned a little feral. "I make my living not cutting to the chase. What's your excuse?"

"That I'm waiting on someone else."

"God help that poor soul," she said, still smiling, flicking her eyes across him once like she was taking his measure for a suit. Then she shook her cigarette until the light went off and vanished into the crowd.

It should have felt like a reprieve. Instead, it felt as though she'd hanged him, wrung him out, and declared him unfit for duty.

He put it aside, tried to even out his breathing. She was the least of his problems. He scanned the room casually, just a guy looking for a slight acquaintance, unconcerned.

To his left, on the raised platform of seating areas, Martine and another girl (Grace, maybe, though he couldn't tell) were crowding a booth, chatting with someone blocked by one of the high-back couches.

Suyana, Daniel thought. His throat went tight.

If Martine had found her, it was over. He should have kept her talking, he should have done whatever it took. Damn, damn, why couldn't he have held it together?

He was so distracted that it took him longer than it should have to register what was going on elsewhere.

There was a tall guy at the bar facing out, a glass in one hand, the other shoved into his pocket. He was fidgeting, leaning away slightly as people pressed in beside him to wave at the bartenders and call for drinks.

Snap. Had to be. No one who belonged here would cede space that easily.

Daniel tried to take comfort that the kid looked less cut-throat than the woman on the phone sounded. He was freak-ishly calm—the only one standing still as the crowd surged against the bar—but he seemed more alert than vicious. Daniel could handle calm and alert. Calm people were prag-matists; they examined situations, they made deals.

Daniel had thought about diplomacy a little, taking photos of Hae Soo-jin pretending to be surprised by visitors. He'd picked up a little about negotiation. The rest he'd picked up since he got here and started shoplifting and handing out bribes.

For a second Daniel wondered if it was possible to get out without catching his attention, but even as he was trying to avert his eyes and keep walking, the guy looked at him and raised his drink.

He'd probably known Daniel was here as soon as he knocked. That was how snaps worked, by knowing everything first. It was why Daniel had wanted to be one to begin with. Felt like a long time ago.

As if Daniel had waved, the guy pushed off the bar and through the crowd, lifting his glass whenever someone's dancing threatened to knock it away. He didn't look at Daniel, which meant he figured Daniel had nowhere to go.

(Daniel thought about the woman who had been on the other end of the phone.)

"You must be Daniel," the guy said when he was close enough. He was older than he'd looked from a distance, with red hair and a square, slightly stolid face, like he'd stepped out of an ad for Alpine health. He held out the glass. "Drink?"

Daniel thought about roofies, seizure-inducers, radium tracking. "Pass."

The guy took a swig. "Figured you could use it, after Martine."

Daniel smiled, thin with no teeth. "Glad you enjoyed the show."

"Didn't stand a chance, man. I've watched her before. You

lasted as long as anyone could." He took another drink. "Of all the people we don't engage, she's the one I'm happiest about."

Daniel looked the guy over, but there were no lapel pins or anything he could peg as a camera. He wondered if there was even anything on him, or if someone else was recording. He glanced around, scanning to see if anyone else was holding too still.

"Do you have a name, or are we just playing with codes?"

The guy smiled. "Bo. And it's not like that. Snaps don't operate like these others. And you're one of us."

That stung.

"Well, at the moment I'm still just a freelance intimidatee, not one of you, so you can understand how I'm wary." Trying to seem like the picture of reason, he said, "I don't even know the company name."

Bo's smile dimmed. "Not without a gesture of good faith, no. I'm under orders, you know how it is." He set the drink down in a corner, then dusted his hands like a man getting down to solving a long-awaited puzzle.

"So," he said, sliding one hand in his pocket, "what can you give me on the target?"

"Nothing."

The rest of Bo's smile disappeared. Nothing else changed, but now he looked a lot less like the picture of Alpine health and much more like a combative weight lifter.

Maybe there was no one else here. It wasn't like Bo needed the backup. Maybe he wasn't even recording, because this was the kind of stuff you didn't want on the record.

Daniel's fingertips went numb.

"Not that I don't want to," Daniel amended as smoothly as he could. "I even came here after her, looking for a story after Ethan was a bust, but she's just not much of a newsmaker."

"I was told you had a good faith gesture," Bo said, as if Daniel hadn't spoken. He and the woman were definitely from the same company.

"Oh," said Daniel, "you mean the—" He reached into his pocket. "I thought you'd expected me to get something between the phone call and now, which is flattering but seems a little optimistic even for your boss."

(Get out, Daniel thought like it would do any good; Suyana, look over here, look over here and run.)

Bo's face softened. "She can be a little brusque," he admitted, "but she gets the goods. It's amazing what she can do."

"You're telling me." Daniel held out the card in two fingers. "I assume that I'll be paid in line with your usual rates. I risked my life for them, it seems only fair."

Bo raised an eyebrow. "She said you'd ask about the bottom line. Half price—on acceptance, obviously—and there are discussions about commission and expenses, if she takes you."

"She'll take me," Daniel said, unable to keep the fatalistic note out of his voice.

The palm-size viewer that had appeared out of nowhere in Bo's hand lit up with two people in an alley, and he slid through them, pausing on the last few frames.

Daniel glanced away. His heart was already pounding fast enough; Suyana bleeding and running from gunfire was the last thing he wanted to see.

"Where's your camera?" he asked, just for something to say, because Bo was distracted and smiling at the pictures as if he'd justified a long night at that long bar, and there wouldn't be a better time to ask.

"What makes you think I'm recording?" Bo asked, sliding back and forth between two frames, but he reached up for a moment and touched his temple, where there was a slight bump with a little scab Daniel hadn't even noticed, scar tissue left over from an old injury. It instantly explained why so many snaps had gotten photos no one should have been able to get.

It made him ill to think about it—how did you know you were getting the shots? How did you record? Could you ever turn it off, or was your whole life a photo essay?

"So," Daniel said, when he could tear his eyes away. "Are we about done, or did you want to buy me a drink?"

He didn't look over at the lounge. If he did, Bo would

look over at the lounge, and there was nothing that camera would miss. Daniel's eyes hurt with not looking. His breath was tight from not looking.

"Sure," said Bo, sliding the viewer in his pocket. "We should talk about what else you can get on Sapaki."

"Nothing."

The word was out before he had a chance to consider a better answer, or a more politic excuse, or a smoother way to make good on an escape.

Bo considered this and then said, calmer than he might have, "This should have been explained to you."

"Yes, it should have been. Instead, all I got were a bunch of amateur threats and some nonsense about spying on a third-rate Face who's done nothing but get shot at."

Bo tilted his head, narrowed his eyes. "She didn't mention you were compromised."

For someone who was supposedly an employee, this woman's name was being safeguarded from him like he was still a threat. Daniel exhaled through his nose, swallowed his answer.

"I understand you develop opinions—happens to everyone," Bo went on, sounding like a guy who had long ago gotten over that little shortcoming, "but if you can't stay objective, we'll tag her with someone else."

"No," said Daniel. Then he added, "That's not the issue.

I was very clear that I was there to photograph Ethan Chambers. If you check with your boss, you'll find out I never agreed to follow Suyana Sapaki."

"You followed her here."

Point. Daniel forced a grin. "If you had a girl like that staring at you like you're a hero, wouldn't you follow her to see if you had a chance?"

"Not really my beat."

"Well, then maybe you'll rescue a handsome guy from gunfire and we'll see how that goes," Daniel said, crossed his fingers in front of his face as if for luck.

He was trying to think of a way to spin this that could get Suyana out of trouble, some other way than being given what he'd always wanted against the one person he'd rather not betray.

After a second he said, as though considering, "What would I be reporting on? I mean, what would you even need her for?"

"Everything," Bo said. "Someone getting shot at tends to be worth following. You must have heard something—you got your picture."

Suyana was moving away from the circle. She was going to duck under the bar and slip out the kitchen entrance and vanish, and one way or another someone was going to get the photo they needed.

"Back in a second," Daniel said. "Champagne goes right through me. We need to talk numbers. If I'm going to follow this, I want enough money to make it worthwhile the next time someone starts shooting."

He slid through the crowd, feeling eyes burning into his back from everyone he passed. His heart thudded against his ribs; he couldn't feel his feet.

Suyana was going to vanish, and the next time he saw her he would be the enemy.

Whether his answer was yes or no, he was going to be a danger to her the rest of his life. This was the least he could do, the last good thing he'd ever manage.

The music thudded against his ribs as he closed the distance between them.

He had ten seconds. It was enough time to warn her.

13

Suyana considered, for one dark moment, how hard she'd have to hit Martine with the tray to break her neck.

She'd refused to kill Ethan, when Zenaida had suggested it as a way of warning the Americans they weren't untouchable. It was possible he had nothing in his favor but her reluctance to kill him, but that was enough. Chordata could push, but she wouldn't be forced. ("I'll talk to Magnus," she'd told Zenaida, knowing he'd jump at the chance to secure their position in a higher echelon by negotiating a relationship with the Americans. Awful, but maybe less awful than killing.)

But there was something about feeling trapped, about being surprised by a hunter, that always made her want to strike.

She said, "Good evening, Martine."

Martine's grin got wider. "I guess you've heard the trouble you're in."

"Magnus was kind enough to tell everyone."

Martine shook her head, ashed the cigarette. It was one of her biggest tells—a small, absent habit left over from the days when she could still smoke—but all it ever heralded was bad news.

"I don't know what you two are doing," Martine said. "Burning you in public is a bit dramatic even for Magnus. You've only been gone a few hours. That's a lot of paperwork just to get back at someone for cheating on you."

She should confirm whatever Martine was saying; any lie was more to her advantage than the truth. But before she could think better of it she said, "No."

Stupid. She knew better than to get angry.

Martine raised an eyebrow. "You sure?"

He thinks of me as a liability, she thought, a strength or a liability, that's all; but just for a moment, there was a warmth on her collarbone where Magnus had rested his fingers.

She filed it away. It was a problem that would hold.

"So if you're not running away from home," Martine pressed, "why did you vanish with some guy?"

This was how Martine won: she got you where she wanted you when there was nothing at stake for her, and let you condemn yourself. Useful lesson, if Suyana lived long enough.

"I vanished because someone was shooting at me."

"Wasn't me," said Martine.

Sometimes Suyana forgot how Martine could cut through the bullshit, when she wanted to.

Grace gave Martine a long-suffering look, then glanced at Suyana. "Do you know who it was?"

Grace said it in a tone that sounded like it was code for *Was it Magnus?* but she and Suyana weren't that friendly, and Suyana couldn't be sure.

"I'm building a list," Suyana said.

"I bet," said Martine. "How long is it, by now?"

"Taller than you, and getting longer."

Martine actually smiled at that, then covered it by taking a puff off her cig.

"I'm hoping to work things out with Magnus," Suyana heard herself saying.

(If he felt that way, was there desperation beneath all this disowning? Martine was probably just sowing discord, but Suyana would take any ammunition she could get.)

"How do you plan to get un-abducted?" Martine asked. "He went public. They can't pretend you're some loser scratching an itch. You're out of the picture. You're working for the enemy until they think of a better story."

Martine wasn't wrong. Her options were narrowing.

Suyana shivered; the glasses on her tray rattled, and she clamped her other hand on it to stop the note from spreading. There wasn't time for panic. She'd have to think of a better story, that was all.

"You're in danger if you stay," Kipa said.

"She's in danger anywhere," put in Grace, looking Suyana over as if this had been a test and her results were disappointing. "Why did you come here?"

"I owed someone a favor," Suyana said.

Grace glanced at Kipa, and some expression crossed her face that Suyana couldn't read.

"Mistake," said Martine. "I don't think you know how much it's worth to turn you in right now."

She didn't sound smug—it sounded like a warning—but Suyana bristled. As if she'd never suffered a swift change of circumstance; as if Magnus had shadowed her from childhood the way Martine's handler Ansfrida had, and hadn't appeared out of the blue, perched on the desk that had belonged to Hakan, whose name had vanished with him.

Acid rose in her throat.

"Call them, then," she snapped. "Prove you're right. Be the person who found me out, that's the cover of *Atalanta* at the very least. And after I disappear, you can hope my replacement never climbs higher than I have."

For just a moment, Martine looked worried, as if she was

trying to determine what deal Suyana had almost sealed that could be fulfilled by her successor.

Good, thought Suyana. A little doubt would be good for her. Let her wonder where Suyana had allied herself before the bullets started.

(Martine's predecessor's predecessor had been the first to sign a relationship contract with the American Face; Martine didn't need that now, but it had been the making of Norway not so long ago, and Suyana guessed it was trivia Martine wasn't allowed to forget.)

"Yes," Martine said. "Let's hope."

Suyana glanced at the door, gauged if she could make it in a sprint before they stopped her, gauged if her leg would make it. At this point, she'd rip the wound open just to get out before Martine could call whatever security guy was slinking around in here on her dime. (Martine didn't trust her well-being to IA-issue bodyguards. All hers were bought and paid for.)

The path was clear. If she could slip out before they stopped her, she might be all right.

Kipa had stopped trembling, as if every moment that went by without someone striking a blow was a good sign and Martine's words were all air. But in Suyana's periphery, she saw Grace hitting a button on something as it disappeared back into her pocket.

That was it, Suyana thought, her stomach dropping out from under her. She'd been called for.

Magnus would be alerted, and in a few minutes whoever he'd appointed would appear through the crowd to bring her outside for a discussion she'd never walk away from.

She measured what was in the balance—anything she could bargain with—and came up with some answers that weren't reassuring.

All right, she thought, set down the tray with shaking hands. If she was marked for death no matter what, she'd scale back her loyalties. If no ideals or politics could give her sanctuary, she could live for her own sake.

It was blind fleeing, it was what animals did when faced with a predator, bolted without strategy or hope—but sometimes there were no choices.

She gave Grace a withering stare, then turned to Martine. (She didn't look at Kipa. Kipa was Chordata's best hope, now that Suyana was out; Kipa was their secret now.)

Martine's grin was two slivers of marble in the dark. "Well, if you're going to run, run."

Pride almost kept her still, but there was no pride in getting caught because someone goaded you. If she was going to die, she wanted to do it more nobly than in a nightclub because she'd been dared to make a point.

She moved for the exit. (She didn't run—that much pride she still had—but it was a near thing.)

Across the club, she saw Daniel heading toward her, his face desperate and grim. She angled back a little to fall into step with him; she'd have a few seconds before she had to duck for the bar and head for the kitchen. It was just enough time for him to tell her something, if he had to.

She kept her eyes forward (the last thing she needed was to alert Martine she knew the taxi dancer), kept her pace steady, primed herself to distinguish his voice amid the hail of voices.

But he reached across her and grabbed her arm. It brought her up short; she spun on her heel to face him. His hand was gripping her just above the elbow, low enough under her gunshot wound not to hurt her.

"Daniel? What—" she started, but his expression was desperate, and he looked as if something terrible was at his heels.

"I'm sorry," he said.

Before she could say anything else he was kissing her. His lips were dry and pressed closed, and he pushed too hard against her mouth—she could feel his teeth. Her mouth had been open; her breath escaped against his teeth. He breathed in through his nose, a sharp, anxious noise. (There had to be a reason for this, this was for someone else's benefit, something was wrong.)

His thumb curled in and pressed too close to the wound, hard enough to bruise; it ached.

Something was very wrong.

She pulled away. He let go at once, as if he'd known, and she saw his neck was strained, his eyes were flat black, he was on the verge of panic.

He said, "Run."

Something moved into her peripheral vision. A shooter, she thought—she took a step back, started to turn.

"Delegate Sapaki," said a stranger.

The screen of the handheld was small (spy-issue, no other reason to have them so small), but it was enough to see herself stepping back from Magnus's hand, moving for the hotel. The picture slid to the next one. She was knocked off balance in it, one arm out and a dark patch on her sleeve, her face a blur.

It was the bullet; he'd taken the photo an instant too late to catch the impact.

Daniel. Daniel had taken it.

She went cold, but there was no doubt in it. That was the angle from the alley, looking out toward the hotel. That was the alley he'd run from to help her.

Whoever this stranger was had his own reasons for showing her, but they were Daniel's work.

She'd known he was a traitor to someone (everyone was).

She'd assumed he would, sooner or later, try to kill her, or turn her over to some faction. Ideals at war led to things like that; it was the nature of the game.

She hadn't imagined so petty a thing as this—so that some snap agency could make a little money. He'd seemed, somehow, to be thinking of better.

It had taken only a moment. When she looked up at him she was still letting out the breath she'd planned to greet him with, and Daniel's face was still empty with shock; no other expression had had time to descend.

She didn't want to think about what she looked like.

She turned and shoved through the crowd, her bad leg burning, fast enough that he'd have to scramble to follow. If he followed her down to the kitchen, she was going to grab a knife and slice his neck open.

Martine was watching Suyana with glittering eyes, her mouth already an O around some insult.

As she passed, Suyana ground out, "He's a snap."

Suyana had just enough time to see Martine's face turn murderous; then Suyana was past the curtains, at the top of the stairs, her mind on what was waiting outside.

Her sense of anonymity had vanished. There were eyes everywhere, trained on her, taking souvenirs. (At least Daniel had taught her something, before he sold her out.)

She pulled the fire alarm.

The music was drowned out by the piercing siren, and the floor rumbled with people heading for the front door—and the back stairs.

She took them double-time. The pain shot up and up and up her leg with every step. Twice she stumbled, grabbed the rail, kept going.

Downstairs, she wedged herself between the barbacks and line cooks pushing toward the exit. They squeezed through two and three at a time, annoyed at the false alarm. If there was really a fire, the kitchen saw it first.

Two of the line cooks had apparently had enough of the evening, and they headed for the corner as soon as they were out the kitchen door. Suyana tried to keep close enough behind them that the cameras would only see a trio of workers slipping out for a drink.

She didn't look around for other cameras. She just had to assume she was being watched, from now on.

There was a pang in her chest. She ignored it.

The crowd was still thick—patrons were sidling and shoving their way out between the waiters. She wondered, with a knot in her stomach, if the panic had given Daniel time to get out before Martine's security tore him to shreds. She couldn't tell which outcome she wanted.

As she turned the corner, it occurred to her that she was looking for a Chordata tail like she was supposed to if there was ever an IA incident. That wasn't true anymore. They didn't even know she was here; nobody but Zenaida had known Suyana and Kipa shared their secret. If someone from Chordata was waiting for her here, she was about to disappear.

Maybe she should do her best to disappear before anything could catch up with her.

Martine was going to call Magnus any second, just for laughs; Daniel had betrayed her in a way that made her sick to think about. It wasn't as though she had much to lose, anymore, by disappearing.

She picked up the pace.

She was two blocks away from Terrain, in a narrow side street deep in shadow, when someone grabbed her arm.

Pain lanced up her shoulder, and it was too dark to see, and Suyana's mind went blank except the cold and furious thought: not tonight you don't.

Suyana stopped suddenly and pivoted as she struck with her free hand as hard as she could. She connected with an arm, knocked it aside. Her attacker yelped.

"Ow! Jesus! I was shouting for you, are you trying to kill me?"

Suyana froze, yanked back the arm that had already been arcing down for another blow.

That voice was no stranger. It was Grace.

14

"Martine made us," said Bo, when they were outside. "We have to go. There's a car waiting."

Unbelievable how calm some people could be.

Take a hint, Daniel thought as they headed down the street. Don't get angry. If you get angry you lose.

"We should talk about what just happened, I think," he managed. His voice sounded a little tight, but it wasn't even a fraction of how he was feeling, which was that he wanted to watch Martine's security guys plant a bullet in Bo's chest.

Bo sighed with the air of a man who'd been recruiting under duress a while. "I did what I had to do to bring you in."

"I have the right to refuse a job offer."

"Usually," said Bo, edged. "But you started this, and you can't get mad that we don't choose the stories."

The crowd was flowing out behind them. Someone was shouldering through, headed their way.

Bo stepped closer. His expression shifted—the false calm vanished, and his words pushed past the cold. "You have nothing, and Sapaki wants you dead. You going to oblige her?"

He'd dropped the act; the words came out bare, and Daniel thought that, not long ago, someone might have dragged Bo from a story he loved by reminding him that snaps had no bridges worth burning.

And when something was laid out by a con man who'd reached the end of his con, a lot of arguments dried up. Sapaki had been a story. The story was over.

(The farther away he kept from her now, the better for both of them.)

"Point," he said, pulled his lips thin like it counted as a smile, and picked up the pace.

If his chest clenched like his ribs were caving in as he slid into the backseat of the waiting car, Daniel figured it was no better than he deserved.

She'd known something was wrong as soon as he kissed her (stupid move, rookie move). It had felt like slow motion as Bo showed up and little disasters cast shadows on her face.

Daniel watched as if from underwater as she realized what had been going on, that whole time she'd let him promise he meant her no harm.

He thought he was prepared for how she'd look at him, until she did. Then he remembered all at once that Suyana dealt with problems, not people, and he was looking at someone who knew how assassinations worked.

It was the best way for her to have looked at him. It would do him good to remember.

The car was new and sleek, and had a fixed barrier between the front and back seats so the driver couldn't snoop. Daniel watched through tinted windows as they slid past groups of people out for the night, groups of tourists hopping lightly from the street to the curb, couples laughing in one another's arms.

"Sorry about that," Bo said.

It was calm, and so vague that Daniel wondered if the backseat was bugged, but there was that same edge of loss that reminded Daniel more than one person could be played in a con like this.

"Not a problem." He tried to summon some charm. After a moment he added, "I'll always remember what you did for me back there."

"I bet." But he didn't move, and he didn't speak to defend

himself, and after another heartbeat he turned to look out his window.

So that's enough, Daniel thought, even though his chest was tight. Be done, until you can do something about it. Fight one thing at a time, if you're planning to win.

He looked out the window and took a couple of breaths, tried to focus. Outside, a knot of girls dressed in sequins sparkled for a moment under a streetlight.

"So," Daniel said, "we're headed to a job interview?"

"You had your interview. We're going to meet the team." Absently, like it was reflex, Bo touched his temple where the camera was.

No wonder Bo had been so careful about what he said. Of course there would be audio. Snaps were always recording. Snaps never missed a story.

To stave off panic, Daniel reminded himself that friend-less wasn't the same as powerless. A snap who joined an agency had advantages; transparency was a decent excuse. A snap could be in a position to profit anytime things fell apart.

Maybe his new boss wanted to see what a young Face would do when you baited her with her worst enemy.

After too long, he said, "All right."

15

Suyana paused outside the car.

Grace frowned. "Problem?" She was anxious, glancing left and right as far as she could without drawing attention. (Faces developed good peripheral vision.)

"A lot of people have put me in the crosshairs in the last twelve hours. I'm sort of hitting the ceiling on people trying to kill me."

Grace's expression cooled a few degrees. "Nice way to accept an invitation."

Suyana didn't apologize. Diplomacy wasn't always politeness. "I'm dog food to the IA. You have more to gain turning me in. Why would I believe you're sheltering me?"

There was a second where Grace seemed confused, as if

she was casting about for the sort of insult Martine would give, if she were here. Then she gave up.

"Yes, you're worth more dead," she said. "But if I've got this right, you've been shot, you can't even walk straight, you're blacklist, and you break into a place full of enemies to warn someone you hardly know."

Now she was facing Suyana over the roof of the car, eye to eye. She looked serious. She looked honest.

Grace said, "That's why."

Something skittered over the roof of the car; Suyana caught it, wondered how tired she was to be catching projectiles. Careless. If it was a grenade, she deserved it.

When she opened her hands, she was holding Grace's comm.

"In case you think I'll call the cavalry," Grace said, and sank into the car. It was enormous; the United Kingdom could afford the best.

Suyana gripped the phone tightly, and followed.

Inside, she started shaking—fatigue. Relief. She crossed her arms, embarrassed Grace might see.

Grace was looking studiously out the window. Suyana would take what she could get.

Dawn was edging over the roofs, and it was light enough to make out faces in the crowd, but Suyana didn't look as the car pulled away; there was no one left to look for.

x x x x x x

Times Suyana Sapaki had met Grace Charles:

At her welcome reception the night before her swearing in, when the Big Nine showed up and had to shake hands with all the new inductees.

During a Women in Politics brunch in New York for teenage girls who won a contest, two years into Suyana's tenure. Everyone gave a statement about how much they loved being a woman in politics. Grace talked wryly about how not everything about being a politician is photo shoots and free food—"Though you should take advantage whenever you can," she said, gesturing at the stacks of pastries on the tables, and everyone laughed. Suyana's was a piece Hakan had gotten approved by someone, about how her involvement in IA politics had opened her eyes to a better world than the one she'd come from. She hadn't read it ahead of time (no point); she had to take a sip of water twice to get through it. When she sat down again at the head table, Grace had handed her a pastry and a Bloody Mary.

In chambers during session, a few times, exchanging careful greetings in the halls.

The annual Gala, when Grace waited until about midnight to start acting sloshed and making loud, laughing conversation with C-listers who didn't understand why they'd been granted the chance but told every joke they had ready.

Suyana had offered Grace a glass of water, the first time, and the act had dropped as Grace raised her eyebrows and took it. She hadn't tried it on Suyana since.

Three open houses Grace threw, over the course of three years. She'd gotten four invitations from Grace this year, but had gone only once; if a C-list said yes to every invitation, it looked like grubbing. Then the explosion had happened back home, and the UARC had fallen off the map, and she'd have gladly grubbed at whatever invitations came, if any had come. Grace's had been first, six months after the explosion; Magnus looked like he was going to cry from relief when he opened it.

In chambers, that morning, when Suyana had voted the way she'd been told, and at the tone of her voice Grace had turned around, just for a second, and looked her right in the eye.

"I'd like to see the lights, please, Paul," Grace said to the driver, after they were on the avenue.

He nodded. Grace pressed a button on her armrest, and a tinted-glass panel rose between them and Paul, until it looked like they'd fallen back into night.

Suyana rested a hand on the door.

"If you're thinking of jumping, don't," said Grace, her archness back in place. "It's just the signal that I'm bringing a girl to the annex." She glanced over, as if she was daring Suyana to disapprove.

Suyana said, "You get an annex?"

A tiny smile flickered across Grace's face, and vanished. "Woman does not live on official quarters alone."

"When we're in session I live in a hotel room, and it's nowhere I'd bring someone back to," Suyana said.

"Colin negotiated it for me a while back. It's out of the surveillance radius." She shrugged. "If I don't let anything interfere with politics, everyone back home is willing to subsidize me seeing a girl or two on the quiet."

"So what, you having a private life depends on you doing what they say?"

She'd meant for it to sound sympathetic, persuasive, but she was too tired, and it came out the way she actually felt about it.

Grace, who wasn't as tired, and was excellent at hiding her real meaning, looked her over. "I'm fortunate enough to be in a position within the IA where I can have some influence over my country's well-being, and I'm willing to be discreet if it means I'm better able to enact change."

Must be nice.

"I did a public service announcement a few years ago," she said. "It was about the importance of agriculture to the global economy, and I thanked America for its contribution. American Farming, Worldwide Growth."

Grace blinked, impassive.

"They had to film it in a wheat field outside Chinon two years back, because the American agricorporate outpost they built outside Aurum back home was burned to the ground, and they couldn't get enough money to build it again. The Americans were threatening to embargo the UARC because of it. That's why I had to do the ad."

Suyana had visited Aurum and toured the outpost with Hakan as an undocumented affair of state, a month before it burned down. She wondered if Hakan had hoped to match her with Ethan back then, too.

She gave Chordata the layout and security notes to destroy the place without loss of life.

(Except Hakan, who vanished into the teeth of the IA, and whoever had died back home when the American investigators came. Zenaida never told her if the UARC lost anyone in the aftermath; collateral damage, she said, when Suyana asked.)

Suyana said, "That PSA was the closest I've ever come to having influence over my country's well-being."

The thing went on heavy rotation on worldwide channels and made her shake with anger every time it aired, and had prevented the embargo; it was really the second closest she'd come, which was the only reason she ever got through it.

(Neither thing had helped her sleep since. Hakan was gone. It was her doing. She could live with it—barely—but that didn't mean it didn't scrape at her in the meantime.)

Grace was looking at her, her dark eyes steady in the false twilight of the car.

"I can't imagine telling the IA how you want to be treated, and then being treated that way," Suyana said, after a while.

The driver turned. They were in an older area of the city now, where nights were quiet. All the shops were shuttered except a florist, just beginning to set out tubs of blooms for the morning.

Grace was looking out the window with a mixture of fondness and distaste as dawn crept over the buildings. She said, "I've found it works best if you have a secret you need to keep, and only ask them for things they're willing to give."

Suyana glanced down at the mobile in her hands that contained Grace's expense account and her top-tier database and her personal stylist's contact and her private-driver intercom and the panic button she hadn't pressed when she saw a blacklisted operative threatening Martine.

Strange, Suyana thought. The United Kingdom was Big Nine. Grace and Martine and Ethan, and the others who had stable economies and agriculture and militaries not given to coups, sat amid the IA chaos without having to worry that their countries would fall apart underneath them.

(When Ethan's camp had sent word back that the USA and the UARC could certainly use better relations, and they'd consider Suyana's offer, a handler had written in the margin: "Ethan thinks she's lovely. —A. Stevens."

It was a strange note to write on a contract where a physical-rights clause was on the table. Even Magnus the unflappable had gotten an odd, tight look on his face as he handed it to her. "Congratulations. I'll tell the stylists not to cut your hair. No point taking chances if he likes you as you are," in the tone that meant he hoped she'd rise to the occasion.

She'd thought it odd that he'd shown her.)

Grace had never had to pray she could catch the eye of a man in power. The United Kingdom was positioned better. Not that Grace would have had to worry; her dark skin glowed in the pink dawn, and even after a long night her eyes were wide and dark and shining. She had the look of a woman born into power she intended to make good use of.

But there was more than one way to suffer. There were at least two IA boys Grace had dated in the last three years (the boy from Russia who'd since aged out, and someone else, briefly. Suyana couldn't remember—Hong Kong Territories, maybe). Had those contracts been carefully negotiated with PDA limits that were humiliatingly explicit about Grace's wishes, or—worse—had she been told to sign the contract as given, and fend for herself?

"Why doesn't Colin just let you date other girl Faces? The IA has plenty."

It had no more impact than a numbers game like that usually would. The only scandal Suyana could think of was that the Icelandic Face and the Swedish Face had been together so long people were starting to think those girls weren't even in a contract.

"Colin and I agreed a long while back that what I do on my own is my own business, and what I do as a Face is the business of the United Kingdom," said Grace, quietly, as if it was something that was often repeated.

Suyana felt someone in Grace's position might be bold, and defy what everyone expected. But the dynamics of power were only obvious in retrospect, no matter how high up you went. And since Suyana, at this time yesterday, had been letting Oona the stylist deep-condition her hair for her meeting with Ethan, she had nothing to say about what people were willing to do when they had to.

Since then she'd been shot, and followed, and blacklisted, and on the brink with the people for whom she'd risked it all, and had trusted a liar because she'd been desperate. She had absolutely nothing to say about how badly things could go wrong for you, if you tried to be bold and failed.

"We're here," said Grace.

Her hand was already on the door as the car slowed, and as soon as it stopped she was outside and moving. For a moment the light reflected off the windows and caught her dress; she was looking left and right, and the sequins on her dress blazed to life. With the next step she fell back into the shadows, and it was snuffed out, and Suyana wondered how many times Grace had hurried into this building with someone she couldn't afford to see again.

Grace stood inside the shelter of the lobby, holding the door for Suyana. As Suyana crossed the threshold, she passed Grace's mobile to her. At the top of the landing, Grace handed it back. She had the start of a smile on her face, as if she wanted to say something kind but knew better.

(They were trained never to give thanks if they were sincere, because if you cared about something, it could be used against you.)

"This wasn't a gallant gesture," she said. "This was so you'd have a fighting chance against whoever comes after you next."

"Wonderful. Thanks."

Grace grinned in earnest. "Let's get upstairs. You need to make sure your wounds are all right, and I want to check in with Colin and see what he knows."

Suyana blinked. This all felt like tripping into a feather

bed at the moment you knew you couldn't take another step.

Please don't be a trap, Suyana thought, examining Grace's expression. Just this once. Please just give me enough room to breathe, that's all.

"All right," Suyana said.

(It meant, "Thank you.")

16

Daniel was silent for a long time as the car snaked though the early-morning traffic. If he was smart, he'd be chatting up Bo. Clearly, snaps had screwed Bo over; knowing how it had happened and making sympathetic faces could have gotten Daniel a friend in the organization, and prevented him from making the same mistakes that had led to Bo doing forcible recruit duty on a Friday night.

That's what you did to sources—you cultivated them, and you milked them for all they were worth, and then you got away as clean as you could.

But somehow he couldn't pull a good front together. He felt empty and ill, like he'd been punched in the stomach on his way out of Terrain, and his mind clicked to a null value over and over.

"We'll get out here," said Bo.

They were on a nondescript corner of a neighborhood of quiet shops and attorneys' or dentists' offices. (Daniel's uncle did his forging from the back of a dentist's office that had once been an attorney's office—you could hardly tell anything had changed.)

The hair on his neck stood up. Don't think about home, he thought. Don't think about anything that happened before right now. You have nowhere to go. You have nothing to fall back on. Swim or drown.

Daniel looked at the still-closed storefronts and the tidy quadrants of streets angling away from them. "So what, I get a blindfold and you spin me around and just push me along until we're there?"

Bo curled his lip. "We're not that kind of organization."

Daniel shot him a look. "You sure?"

"To your left," Bo said, long-suffering.

He definitely should have asked what mistake Bo had made that landed him with this backwater beat. Bo couldn't be older than thirty—he shouldn't sound eighty. Suyana might think Daniel was the scum of the earth, but Daniel was too good at what he did to get trapped in rookie-babysitting duty, that was for sure.

Daniel slid his hands in his pockets and started walking. The necklace scraped his knuckles, bit into his fingers when he gripped it.

"Stop," Bo said, in front of a slightly shabby window that read BONNAIRE ATELIER. Two headless mannequins decorated the storefront; one was wearing a hideous wedding dress, the other had on half a blazer that was chalk-marked and missing a sleeve.

Daniel frowned. "Does this fool anyone?"

Bo didn't answer.

Past the counter was the door to the service stairwell, which Bo locked behind them. Daniel turned and headed down.

"Wrong way."

Daniel was impressed. It took a real entrepreneur to put the offices of her black-market agency on the upper floors of a building, where surveillance by the opposition was much easier to come by.

That meant she didn't like being in places where there was only one way out. Worth knowing.

Bo led the way up the stairs, and unlocked the door on the second floor that led into the entrance hall of a flat. It was meticulously decorated. The sitting room had mismatched velvet sofas and tables adorned with lamps and sculptures and stacks of art books. There were sideboards against the walls (one with a television), and a dining table with an upholstered chair at the head of it that looked like a throne. There was a little kitchen that had never been used, and a washroom.

On the far side was a closed door, and just looking at it made Daniel's fingertips go numb with dread. She could decorate in glamorous disarray all she wanted, but Daniel knew this wasn't a flat anyone lived in.

It was a war room.

"She's expecting us," Bo said, and knocked.

And either Bo must have been higher up on the food chain than Daniel thought or his new boss knew everyone who crossed her doorstep, because Bo didn't wait for a response before he opened the door, and she was already saying, "Daniel will meet you in the shop, Bo, thank you."

Bo looked over at him and raised an eyebrow.

Daniel shrugged, crossed the rest of the sitting area, and stepped inside.

The room had been meant as a bedroom, once—there was even a fireplace—but it was a stronghold now. There was a monstrous desk stacked on one side with tech; a small chair sat empty in front of it, and behind it, she was waiting.

He'd pictured her in a huge curved chair that turned slowly to reveal her, like a villain in a movie. But it was just an office chair, and she was already facing him, her hands laced together on the desk, her gaze exactly at his eye level even before he was in sight.

There hadn't been any cameras in the windows of the shop. They must have been in the mannequins, and she'd gauged his height from that. He took it back about the storefront not fooling anyone.

"Have a seat," she said.

He did. What else was he supposed to do?

She wore bright red lipstick, seemingly an inch thick, its lines perfect; the collar of her black suit curled at the edges, and her hair was pulled back, and if he had to guess he'd put her in her late thirties with the confidence of someone who'd killed that many.

"You must be thirsty," she said, and set a bottle of water, still sealed, within his reach.

Her voice wasn't as low as he remembered from the phone call, but he'd been remembering a monster. In this well-appointed office in the early-morning light, the words were alto and round and clear as a bell, and he imagined she'd done her share of recruiting at this desk, with a voice like hers.

But he had no name to put to her voice, because she still hadn't given him one, so he sat back and crossed his legs like he was actually comfortable, and reminded himself she was the enemy.

"We haven't met," he said.

She smiled without parting her lips. "Li Zhao," she said.

"Owner of Bonnaire Atelier, Bonnaire Fine Tailoring, and Bonnaire Workshop."

Bo hadn't been a very informative hostage-babysitter. Daniel didn't even know where the other two places were. One in New York, he guessed; maybe London. Maybe Hong Kong. Maybe it was one name for each continent where she had countless snaps crossing borders twenty-four hours a day.

"I've seen your work," Daniel said. "Not sure I like some of your methods."

"I'm not sure I do either, but as long as they keep working, I'll keep using them."

"How often do you threaten people's families just to get them to come in and meet you?"

She raised an eyebrow. "Funny thing. Most snaps are happy to meet with us, so you're the first in a while where I've had to apply pressure."

Like a wound, Daniel thought.

"But honestly, I wasn't worried. Your family seems like nice people, and I had a feeling nothing would have to get ugly. You strike me as a reasonable man."

He almost said, *Why are you talking to me like I'm your brother?* but he stopped himself. You came this far without anyone else, he thought; you have defenses. Use them. Don't let this be the end of the line.

"I'm trying to be a reasonable man. I can't say the same

for the guy you sent to fetch me. I hope his recruitment skills aren't indicative of the company."

She turned to something on her computer. "I gave Bo a task, and he did what it took. That's very indicative of this company." She said it coolly, though her mouth was just barely turned up, a red crescent just at the edges.

"Bo's strong-arming probably drove Suyana Sapaki into an assassination attempt," he said. "That's pretty involved behavior for a snap."

"If Bo pushed Sapaki into danger, he'll have to live with that. But that's between Bo and the story he's willing to settle for, and frankly, I'm not sure you get to say very much about being nosy."

She angled one of her monitors so he could see it. He steeled himself to look at a shot of the kiss. But it was a shot of Café de Troyes—grainy from exposure, and fuzzy in one corner where a streetlight had bled into the feed.

He was distracted, and it took him a second to see that he and Suyana were coming out the door. He was so close behind her the hem of his coat was brushing her leg. She was looking down the street, focused, determined. He was looking at her.

His expression didn't bear thinking about.

"I know it's strange to be on the other side of the lens," she said, with real sympathy.

Ice slid up his spine. Daniel wanted to look up at her, look her in the eye, see where she was going. He didn't dare.

He reevaluated some things in the few seconds it took for him to be able to breathe again.

"I was after a story with all this, you know," he said. He forced himself to sound as disconnected as he could. He was lying, and they both knew it, but sometimes you just really needed to try out the lie. "It was shaping up, too, before Bo dragged me off-site in a fit of pique."

"You're too close to that story," she said in a cut-the-shit voice, sitting back. "It will be reassigned. But your instincts are good—you got further than most amateurs would have. It helps that you're without compunction."

She said it without fanfare, as if it was an advantage he couldn't help, like being tall.

"Thanks," he said. Then, "Reassigned?"

"When she left Terrain, she was still all right. So long as she can keep herself alive, we'll watch her."

Daniel frowned. She sounded almost proud of Suyana; almost excited about her.

And someone would be looking after Suyana, then. She wouldn't be alone. That was something. Maybe it was best that it wasn't him. The knot of her necklace hung heavy in his pocket.

"I see."

Li Zhao shot him a look. "You may not like my methods, but what we do is more important than that. The story you brought us is important."

"I agree," he started, but when she looked at him, he closed his mouth over the rest.

"Whether or not Sapaki lives," she said, "there are alliances that will break because of this, and probably a colonial occupation, and the IA would rather no one know about it in time to get angry."

Jesus. "Who would colonize?"

"The usual suspects. All of whom have press corps that will fight to keep their countries' secrets, because that's what they're trained to do. You won't hear a word about this from them."

She looked at him level. "The free press is gone, except for us. And both sides would be happy to see the end of us, except that they benefit too much from us to risk it."

He had questions about the safety of this pitch, and even more about propaganda of this pitch, but still, he was holding his breath.

She leaned forward. "It's complicated, to do what we do. Sometimes it's dirty work, and sometimes people die. We don't get involved. That's the cost of doing business."

Before he could think better of it, he said, "So why are you so happy Suyana Sapaki isn't dead yet?"

She blinked. After a second, the shadow of a smile crossed her face.

"It's always nice to find a diplomat with something going on under the shell. We started following Hae Soo-jin after she showed initiative—though she'll never get away with that again."

Daniel swallowed. "Did they—?"

"No. They didn't dare try retirement. They didn't want to admit they didn't know who else she knew. She's been training her replacement since everything broke. We've been doing a brisk business selling candids of her to her own team. Nothing's come up."

"And if it had?"

Another question too blunt to get a good answer—the problem with being caught off guard. He suspected she wouldn't have sold it, but it would be good to know there were limits, for Suyana's sake.

"Seems a bit late to worry about that," she said.

He had no argument. He scraped the pad of one finger with his thumbnail.

"Sapaki's done something worth killing her over, and she survived it. It's shaping up to be a better story than we could have anticipated."

His stomach twisted. "Do you know who tried to kill her?"

She shook her head, glanced at her computer screen as something flickered across it. "The shooting brought her to our attention. Before that we didn't think there was much to follow. We investigated just after the big Chordata strike, of course, but nothing surfaced."

The Chordata strike she'd catalyzed, he thought, tried hard not to look proud of her.

"But you knew there would be a story, before there was one." She was looking at him sidelong. "You found it, and you followed it. Someone who can scout talent is worth recruiting."

She thought of them as talent. She thought this was recruiting.

Surveillance on Faces, pictures sold to a market you couldn't control, pinpointing stories before they broke, a lifetime of taking photos hoping you weren't toppling a government—or hoping you were. It had sounded like a good idea when he was angry and on the run and hoping to catch a few pictures of Faces dating on the sly. He wasn't sure he could handle a lifetime of this.

But there weren't many other places that were going to extend him any protection at all. One day didn't change something like that. You don't have options.

"We're not the bad guys," Li Zhao said. "Well, not the worst guys. Work with us. Keep a few rich people honest. Scare some good behavior into the wicked. It's honest work, as lying goes."

He had no reason to fight it. He hadn't changed so much in two days that he couldn't recognize an opportunity when it kidnapped him.

He said, "Where do I get started?"

17

As soon as they were inside, Grace toed off her shoes and unhooked her earrings. "Unzip me, would you? Then we'll get you out of sight. I need to talk to Colin and he shouldn't know you're here."

Colin would know Grace had brought someone home, of course, but the driver hadn't recognized Suyana. Daniel hadn't followed her; Chordata didn't know where she was. There was a chance that she was, for the moment, invisible.

She'd make the most of it.

The flat was a cramped studio, with a bed and a table with two junkyard chairs and one cutting-edge viewscreen slapped to the wall that might as well have been labeled

I AM TETHERED TO MY WORK. The UK might be willing to let Grace have the place, but they didn't want her getting cozy and forgetting her duties.

Grace slid out of her dress and grabbed a shirt from under one of the pillows. "There isn't much place to hide. You want to be behind the bed or in the bathroom?"

"The bed," said Suyana. From there it would be harder to lock her in.

She wanted (she hoped) to have time to breathe here, but it had been an educational day and she was prepared. She'd already seen the garden wall and guessed how far a drop it was, if she had to jump.

Grace slid her shirt over her head; it fell halfway to her knees. "So, what got you shot at, Amazonian?"

There was a tricky question.

"I was meeting a boy."

Grace glanced sidelong. "The boy who kissed you at Terrain?"

"No," Suyana said.

"Oh. Who was that one?"

"A snap." The word scraped her throat; her eyes were fixed, unseeing, out the window.

Grace made a face. "Well, for a snap he has some flair. Hopefully Martine didn't kill him."

"I think Martine was too busy enjoying the moment before she called Magnus on me."

Grace shrugged. "You'd be surprised about Martine."

She moved out of Suyana's line of sight, and there was the sound of a refrigerator opening and closing, and something being poured into a glass. "How did he rate?"

Suyana felt heavy and miserable thinking about it, the jarring feeling everywhere even though they were only touching in two places.

"I wouldn't know," Suyana said.

He'd been her first kiss. A traitor. No worse than signing it away to Ethan Chambers over a contract lunch, but it didn't say much for her taste.

"What? You're joking. Magnus can't find you someone to practice dates with?"

Grace said it as if it was a surprise.

"I don't date."

"You've never struck out on your own?"

"You just saw it."

Grace came back with a glass of water for herself and handed Suyana a bottle, still sealed.

Grace said, "It's a bit frowned upon to go on dates as if they're business meetings and have sex like a contractual obligation. These relationships only work in your favor if the delegation stays happy and the public buys that you're interested. You don't really have to be, of course—you shouldn't be—but there's an art in the artifice."

Suyana didn't doubt it, especially coming from Grace.

"I practice the art of seeming all right with Magnus as my handler," she said. "That's enough work."

"But he's never brought in someone? No outsiders to cut your teeth on?"

"No."

Grace raised an eyebrow. Suyana frowned.

"You don't have to look at me like I'm the one who shot you," Grace said. "It's interesting to see how people's patterns betray them. That's all."

"Mine or his?"

Grace half smiled. "His, but stick around and I'll tell you yours, too."

Suyana knew her own patterns already. They didn't say much she wanted Grace to know. (Foolish and stupid and out of options; not much of an ally.)

"I'll get out of sight," she said. "You should call Colin."

Easing herself down to the floor shot a bolt of pain up her arm, and she bit back a groan.

"Should you be at a hospital?"

"I ran away from one already."

Grace looked at her like she was out of her mind. Suyana would grant that. It had been a long day.

She settled in where she could look obliquely at the reflection of the viewscreen in the window.

Grace pressed her fingertip to the scanner, and a moment later the secure-connection icon appeared, and Grace was looking at Colin.

He was middle-aged, and his skin was a shade darker than Grace's, and he looked just as he did when Suyana saw him on the IA floor: focused and kind. His office was piled high with papers, and his tie was pulled askew just enough that he looked harried despite himself.

When he saw Grace his face relaxed even though he was frowning, something deep and worried that vanished as soon as he saw her well.

"You know, Ansfrida heard from Martine nearly an hour ago, and it's not as though Martine is a pillar of punctuality. Next time you flee a nightclub fire with a stranger, you might want to contact me sooner."

"Paul knew I got in all right. Surely he called."

"I don't trust Paul as much as I trust you. And you haven't contacted me all day. We have things to go over."

"At this hour?"

"Iceland got back to us about the geothermal energy contract, you're confirmed for the photo shoot and interview with *Closer* next week, and we need to talk about how we're going to handle the renewable-energy snarl before they bring it up in committee."

"Lovely. Thanks for the scintillating update."

Colin gave the screen a face. "Have you heard what happened to Suyana Sapaki?"

"Not much."

Despite being so tired it hurt just to breathe, Suyana had to smile. Grace was a consummate actress.

"She's gone missing," Colin said. "Magnus thought it was just Sapaki acting out, and the shooting business was a cover, but when the Committee approached him to confirm, he was low on evidence. They told him to proceed as if it was a kidnapping and cut all ties. No idea where she is."

Something about it tugged at Suyana, somehow. Ethan had been her idea. Magnus knew she wouldn't skip out. Had he been covering for her in a bid to keep her from getting burned by the IA Committee? Had she underestimated his loyalty?

"Goodness," said Grace.

Colin paused a moment before he said, "Yes, it's very upsetting."

Was that a code word? Had he hesitated because he knew? Had Grace betrayed her? Suyana clenched her good hand into a fist, fought the urge to stand up and run.

"Please be careful," Colin said. "Magnus seems very cagey. I'm not at all certain he believes what the IA told him. He seems sure she's alive, but he's concerned."

"Concerned" meant action. Magnus was looking for her; Magnus wasn't the type to give up.

Colin was shaking his head. "I don't think Sapaki would have planned something like this, and even if Magnus is telling the truth," in a tone that suggested this was unlikely, "there might still be Faces in danger. I wish you'd come back so we could keep an eye on you."

"I'll come home soon."

Colin leaned forward an inch. "I'll send the car for you now if you like."

Pushy, Suyana thought, but couldn't tell if it was out of concern or control.

Grace gave the screen a significant look. "I'm hosting a guest, Colin. We have plans. Shall I bring her with me?"

"You know I don't care."

"So we'll come in, then?"

"Grace, the home office—"

"Wants to save me for men they can use. You've said."

It was pointed. There was a little pause.

Colin sighed. "Stay there for the moment, then. It might be best to be out of the way until we know what happened to Sapaki. If Magnus tries you, don't answer."

"Wolf at the door?"

He smiled; it wavered a little in the reflection, as Suyana struggled to keep her eyes open.

"More like a desperate man begging for a new post, if this goes poorly. I'd just as soon not be deposed by some scrabbling diplomat half my age, thanks."

He was underestimating Magnus.

"Keep me posted, please, Grace. You have your jewelry?"

He meant the comm bracelet; Grace gave the vid screen a fond and put-out glance.

That's the sort of silly joke a father makes, Suyana thought. A pang of regret sliced through her. She knew it was only this sharp because she was so worn down, but it felt as though a rib had broken.

Her father died when she was young. She hadn't seen her mother more than a handful of times in the years since someone sent Hakan to ask her some questions.

(There had been moments, early on, when she'd tried to look at Hakan as a father. Didn't work, but it was easier, sometimes, to pretend you were loved.)

"Good night," said Grace. "Go home."

"Home?" Colin was smiling. "Whatever do you mean?"

Grace rolled her eyes and severed the connection.

Suyana felt strangely obvious. She'd eavesdropped on a hundred conversations between Faces and handlers in chambers, but that had felt like a professional skill. This felt like she'd walked in on a family call.

"He seems to actually like you," Suyana said.

"He says that," Grace said, lifted and dropped one shoulder. "Sometimes I want to believe him, but it's best not to. You never know."

If you asked her, Colin had the look of a man with a daughter. Though, just now, Grace had the look of a woman with a father. Theirs wasn't a trusting business.

Suyana didn't know if it was worse to let someone get one over on you, or to throw away real feelings. It seemed such a sin, not to believe the truth when it was handed to you; it was a rare enough thing.

If she was being honest, she'd err how Grace had erred. Better go out too cold than go out a fool. She'd tried to imagine Hakan as a father, and look what it had done to him.

"Anyway," Grace said as if Suyana had argued, "it doesn't matter. I'll expire any day now. I know they're looking, Colin gets messages all the time about someone new that they've taken an interest in. It's just a matter of finding someone with the story they're looking for. They'll write me right off stage." She sighed and tugged at her bottom lip. "I need to start smoking or something."

"Martine would say you were copying."

Grace glanced over and smiled. "Didn't realize you knew Martine."

Suyana thought everyone knew Martine. Martine made

sure everyone knew. But Grace was looking at her as if Suyana had seen deeper than she should have seen.

"It's just a guess."

Grace looked her up and down. "You never said what you were warning Kipa about."

Suyana actually thought about confiding. Maybe Grace would be in her corner. She'd be an asset. She had the power to change things. Colin, the mouth of England, might have her personal life on a leash, but when she stood up in the IA, the cameras were always, always on.

Then again, Suyana had trusted someone else about it, because she'd hoped for the best. Don't repeat mistakes; unforgivable. She slid the impulse to confide where it could never touch another thing, locked it shut.

"No, I never did."

Grace's face hardened. "I've done a pretty significant opening volley, here. It's best practice to reciprocate."

"This is safe with me."

"But not worth anything in return."

That wasn't true, they knew it wasn't. Grace had shown Suyana something that could end Grace's career.

But at worst, that meant Grace went home with a pension and lived mostly anonymously in some city that saw its share of washed-up celebrities, and every once in a while someone from the press would hound her for a wistful quote about her fall from the IA's upper echelons.

Suyana had no fallback. She was enough of a liability that they'd replaced her handler to keep her in line.

(Magnus, who took his job seriously. Magnus, who was looking for her on radio channels no one talked about.)

She'd been arranging an affair with the American because without a friendship to call on, the last pretense of home rule in her country would vanish. She'd been prepared to sleep with a stranger for the public eye, while she ransacked his offices and passed information to the people who would do what it took to prevent the last of the green from going. And someone who knew about that had shot her twice.

She looked up at Grace.

"It's worth your life," she said, "what I know."

It was an offer. Grace thought it over.

Suyana watched some conflicts flicker across the face of a natural diplomat with the same envy she always had when she was around those born to their work. They learned to weigh risks with an ease you never quite managed if you came late and had to negotiate power from the bottom.

"That's a different kind of best practice," Grace said finally. "Keep it. Let me know what I can do."

Suyana let out a breath of relief. Then she had to catch herself on stiff arms to keep from falling backward; her adrenaline had vanished, and her strength with it.

Safe. She was safe, here, for a little while. She had to go soon—Chordata needed to know about Daniel. But she couldn't think about it; it wasn't the kind of thing you had the courage to do, if you thought about it much.

"You could get me gauze and antiseptic, if you can stomach first aid on bullet wounds. And I need caffeine." Her vision was starting to get bright clouds just at the edges, whenever she moved.

Grace looked her over. "When was the last time you slept?"

She'd passed out back in Montmartre, before the hospital. And she'd closed her eyes for a little while in the narrow bed with Daniel, trusting where she shouldn't have trusted. Maybe as she slept he'd lain beside her, taking notes for the cover story this would make.

She'd need a corpse to point to, if she was ever getting back home. Daniel's was at the top of the list.

"I'll manage," she said.

"I don't mean this unkindly, but honestly, it doesn't look it. We'll clean your wounds, and then you should get a few hours of sleep. Seek vengeance in the morning."

Grace said it archly, but her eyes were serious and still.

Suyana was shaking with exhaustion, and she could feel her fingers trembling against her legs even where she stood braced against the wall. If she were wearing any jewelry, she'd be rattling.

"I have to be on the move by nightfall."

It was capitulation. Grace smiled. "Sit down. I'll see what I have in the cupboard."

Suyana sank onto the bed. Immediately, pain slid from her feet through her calves, sharp and red and throbbing. The gunshot wound itself had gone past painful to numb, and she decided not to look at it until she had to. It would probably be all right. The wound was clean, mostly. It hadn't come through the bone.

(It was a flesh wound, and not a shattered bone, because Daniel had moved into the gunman's view when he ran out to help her and muddied the shot.)

When she tried to tug her sleeve free of the dried blood, she yelped through clamped teeth, and for a moment there was an explosion of sparks behind her eyes.

She thought about how cramped and tired she'd been yesterday afternoon, someone else's pricey necklace weighing on her, Magnus not quite looking at her all the way up to the hotel to meet Ethan, and Daniel crouched in the alley filming it all. It felt like years ago, like she'd been wading through someone else's mistakes.

She cut that train of thought short. That was fatigue. If there were mistakes, they were hers; if she was going to survive, she had to stop thinking about things it was too late to change.

It was getting harder to think, anyway; how cloudy her mind was now, how it was like an empty boat on the river, knocking against the shore with no purpose or power.

She was dizzy, she realized, now that it was quiet enough to focus; her spine was gnarled. She had to roll up her pant leg to find the wound. She had to lie down for a moment, just until her arms were strong enough to reach. Almost against her will she stretched across the bed, which smelled like hotel sheets.

Something tugged at her—something about that was dangerous, wrong.

But she was falling fast, crashing so hard into sleep it stung her fingertips and her eye sockets, and whether Grace brought back first aid or had a knife in her hand to finish the job, Suyana couldn't tell.

18

When Daniel came out of Li Zhao's office, Bo was waiting, hands in his pockets, rocking on his heels like he hadn't expected to be waiting long.

It cut Daniel to the quick, somehow, that the guy who'd ruined his life a few hours ago was still treating this like a babysitting gig.

"I must have been a sure thing."

Bo shrugged. "Not much to lose," he said. "I figured she wouldn't have to fight too much to get you on board."

It was an honest answer, but it lacked a certain comfort.

Bo turned. "Let's go downstairs and meet some of the tech team."

"Downstairs" turned out to be a warren of rooms in the basement, which you reached via lift behind a bookcase in the flat (of course you did). As they entered, Daniel realized the space was big enough to be encroaching under the buildings left and right (there were closed doors that must lead elsewhere—maybe they'd just gone for the brass ring and eaten up an entire city block of cellars).

Computer screens stood in banks on sharp white desks with open steel cabinets beneath them, drives whirring.

So all their data came to Li Zhao's people in real time, with no lag or download or opportunity to tamper. That was depressingly informative.

The whole place was lit with crisp fluorescents, except for an open sitting area in one corner illuminated with brass floor lamps standing sentinel behind couches. Li Zhao must have insisted there be some space down here that didn't look like where robotics went to die.

There was no photography equipment on any of the shelves, and it took Daniel a second to remember why.

"Kate, Dev," Bo said. "We have a recruit."

Two heads appeared from behind monitors along a bank of desks at the back of the room. The girl had black hair and earrings along the edge of both ears; the boy was cast a little green in the monitor glow, and his glasses looked like two independent screens hovering in front of him.

"Well, I'll be damned," said Kate. "You owe me twenty."

Dev pulled a face and reached into his pocket. "We didn't set a time frame defining success. If he washes out in six weeks that doesn't count."

"Certainly something for you to learn from, but irrelevant to the subject at hand," said Kate, stretching out her arm to snag the cash.

"The subject wants to know what the bet was, exactly," Daniel said.

Kate grinned in a way that made Daniel a little nervous. "Whether Bo could find you and bring you in before the week was out," she said.

"Unfortunately that was the whole bet," said Dev. "Don't wash out, please, or I've wasted a twenty."

Bo was frowning at both of them. "You thought it would take me until the end of the week?"

"Don't look at me," said Kate. "Dev's the nonbeliever."

Dev raised his eyebrows, long-suffering, at Bo.

"Guess I should have put up more of a fight," Daniel said.

He'd thought a warm welcome would be better than not, but the idea that he had been somebody's side bet left a bad taste in his mouth. He'd already been somebody's side bet once. He wasn't eager for a reminder.

"Not worth it," said Kate. "It would just make it harder

to be where you are now." She was back to looking at her screen, and her fingers were flying over the keys.

Dev frowned over at her. "What are you doing?"

"Telling the others."

Daniel blinked. "How many of you are there?"

"We're the third watch," said Dev. "And then the off-sites."

Off-sites. Tailoring and Atelier and everything else, plus backup in an undisclosed location, with another set of eyes. Well.

The good news was that no one would ever miss giving him credit for a story he broke. The bad news was that he was starting to itch just thinking about it.

"Mention how hard I fought," Daniel said.

One corner of Kate's mouth turned up. She never stopped typing. Dev's glasses flickered as he scanned through photos.

"Do I get a tour of the goods?"

Bo and Kate exchanged looks. Then Kate shrugged and swiveled a monitor toward him, turned her wheelchair to face the computer from the new angle. She had silver braces on her legs, sleek and gleaming as the rings laddered up her ears.

"This is it," she said, about an interface that looked like it could pilot a starship. "Here's our feeds, facial recognition scanning for untagged subjects, date stamper, snap ID and location, captions are for Watch notes."

"Can I see?"

Kate shot him a look. Her eyes were black in this light, and keen. "Sure."

She hit a button, and a thumbnail blew up in the center of the monitor. It was the picture he'd taken of Suyana getting shot. He forced himself not to react.

This big, he could see it was the moment after the shot, when her shock had faded and horror was dawning; the moment she must have thought she was going to die.

Underneath it was an ID number and the date, and a slug line: *PARIS: SUYANA SAPAKI, F-UARC, shot by unknown assailant. Out of frame—Magnus Samuelsson (handler), Daniel Park (snap). NOTE: Park intervened after this photo was taken. Mixed results.*

There were reference numbers—probably to the frames where his focus was off, because he'd already been lowering the camera, realizing he had to do something.

"The note's a bit much."

"We're watching feeds for eight hours a day," Dev said, unconcerned. "You get editorial."

"It's not just you," Kate said. The photo vanished into a sea of photos scrolling past, being cataloged in real time. He saw a few other pictures of Suyana at public events before the feed expanded to include other Faces, their events speeding by, the search moving outward in fractals.

There was quite a bit of Martine over the transom. In every shot, she seemed like she knew she was in front of a camera, but he couldn't tell if she was onto them or that was just how she looked.

If he was being honest, he'd admit there was something visceral about looking at the sheer volume of secrets that Bonnaire Atelier and Fine Tailoring was holding on to. This was unfiltered, live, prime evidence from fifteen countries, each photo waiting for the right moment to trap a hypocrite or sink a shady deal or tip the scales of public opinion.

People in charge were only ever honest when they thought they were being watched. And there was a sea of watchful waiting power, right in front of him. All he had to do was be willing to give in; be a part instead of a whole.

He felt, for just a second, what Suyana might have felt in the moment before she crossed the stage and became the Face of her country.

"Wait, wait," he said, blinking back to attention and leaning in. "Hold there a second?"

"A born snap, can't mind his own business," Kate said, but she scrolled back a few frames.

At first he wasn't sure what about the photo had arrested him. It was a crowd scene—no real motion. Groups of people were laughing and talking. To the right of the frame, a blonde in a hat was talking to a man with dark hair.

Maybe her expression had been what caught his eye—amid the smiles, her face was drawn, her mouth slightly downturned.

The crowd was pressed in close around the edges of the lens, and her profile was slightly out of focus, but Daniel finally recognized Margot, head of the IA Central Committee.

It took him a moment, though. On the magazine covers that usually featured her (*Elan*, sometimes the *Weekly Global*) she was so carefully styled she looked like an Impressionist painting. Here her hair was pulled sharply back, her face shaded by the brim of her hat.

She'd been the Committee head who shook Suyana's hand when Suyana crossed the stage in her ugly dress to accept her post, all those years back. He'd watched it a dozen times. If it weren't for that, he might not have known Margot at all.

The man had dark hair, and someone's hairdo in the foreground was obscuring part of his profile, but still, something about that face set off some alarm bell. He didn't know why. His heart thudded against his ears.

After a second he managed, "Who took these? How do you even find Margot?"

Kate shot a look over her shoulder. "Bo did. He hunts big game."

"Yeah, great, thanks," said Bo, smoothing down his hair self-consciously. But he didn't argue the point, and he looked at the photo with a certain focus, as if he could remember exactly what the air had smelled like the moment he took that picture.

Daniel asked, carefully casual, "What was she talking to this guy about?"

Kate keyed up the video, but it was a wall of crowd noise, and their voices were lost.

"When did you say these were taken?"

"Five, six days back," Bo said. "Before I got assigned to recruitment duty."

Daniel shot a grin over his shoulder. "I'm your best work of the week, then."

Dev choked. Kate's eyes were wide as she rolled back to her station and pointedly turned the monitor away from him.

Bo said, "You have a lot of confidence for a guy who doesn't know who's putting his camera in."

Shit. "Point. Sorry. Don't let me bleed to death, please."

"No hard feelings," Bo said after a moment. "Let's get your camera lined up, then. As soon as you're done we'll get going. There's work we need to do."

Bo vanished behind one of the open doors like a film of smoke, and even when the light went on in the little exam room, it took Daniel a second to place where Bo was inside it. He needed to stop snapping at Bo. Bo was six inches taller than Daniel and could disappear in a room in which he was the only occupant. He'd have to learn how to be invisible. Bo was a good teacher.

This was what he wanted, Daniel reminded himself. This was what it took.

He'd handled his passage; he'd handled the theft of a camera worth half what his passage had been; he'd handled setup for his first assignment alone. He could handle this.

"Nice shot," Dev said to his computer. "Kate, it's headed your way."

A moment later, Kate said, "Oh, nice. Put it with the personals."

"Can I see?" Daniel leaned over. Three figures were standing together in the narrow alley between a noodle place and a shabby, low-rent temple; there was a smear of neon filtering in from one corner, left over from the camera turning away too quickly from a sign. It was a good picture—it suggested a story about the people in it.

"What are they talking about?"

"Doesn't concern you," said Kate.

"Well, I'll know when whoever's in this picture gets busted." He peered closer, trying to figure out who exactly was in it.

Dev smiled. "That's the problem. Doesn't matter how it looks. You want confirmed IDs first, everything else second.

Sometimes we get to pass on a great shot right to the papers, but most of the time ..." He waved his left hand vaguely as he moused the photo back into the stream it had come from.

"So we don't try to make it look good?"

Dev looked at him a second. Then he said, "That's not really the job description."

Daniel couldn't decide if it was better or worse not to have much say about which frames made it into the world. He knew how to take a picture, but that was a job for photographers; he was a just a walking camera now.

"Go ahead, Bo, I've keyed it," said Kate. "He's 35178."

In the other room, Bo was lifting a pill out of a metal canister.

"Oh no," Daniel murmured.

"It hardly hurts," said Dev.

His voice was kind. Daniel looked over. Dev smiled and tapped his temple, where there was a bump so small Daniel had missed it.

"I'm just feeling sorry for my poor handsome face," Daniel said.

"Don't worry," said Kate without looking up. "We'll still get to see it every time you look in a mirror."

The hair on his neck stood up.

The idea of it filled his mind as he took the chair in the operating room, and Bo injected the anesthetic, and even in the moment before he fell into the twilight sleep and remembered where he'd seen the man in the photo, his dreams caught on the image of him looking into the mirror and seeing an empty face, save the little black mole and the camera's whirring eye.

19

Suyana dreamed of the forest.

It sat waterlogged, dark and green and teeming with life, filled with the screeches of birds and monkeys and the little clicks of insects and the falls like thunder, far away.

The forest was always a good dream.

She'd only seen it once, that first year when the IA was taking a picture for her official card. All the rest of her work had been listening to drunk Faces complaining at Terrain and handlers fighting in offices that were never as sound-proof as you thought, and interns who were too busy to shred things for an hour after they were told to. Her envi-ronmental revolution was walking through *parfum* at the department store, talking to a woman she pretended wasn't a stranger.

She'd been working for years for a place she couldn't remember when her eyes were open. When she did, it was mixed up with the idea of Chordata being too fractured to hold on for long (a bureaucrat's worry), worries about Zenaida, worries about being caught, Hakan's face every time he looked at her like he was wondering whether to ask her and make her lie.

But now she stood at the edge of the canopy, ferns tickling her hand as she knelt to touch the ground. The wind in the trees, and the sound of water, and green things all around her growing and safe; it was a good dream.

She woke up not knowing where she was.

It was a hazard of the trade. Faces went where they were told. She was used to it; it hadn't panicked her for years. It helped remind you that you had to be careful, that you were playing a part from the moment you opened your eyes.

But just because it was helpful didn't make it a comfort, and Suyana fought the stomach-sinking moment of disorientation. She kept her eyes closed for a heartbeat, listening for anything that might ground her.

There was someone next to her, breathing quietly.

For a moment, her body flooded with panic. Then she

remembered. By the time she opened her eyes, she knew it was Grace asleep beside her.

It was strange, impossibly strange; she felt as if the bed were sinking though she was perfectly still. Maybe this happened once you were in a relationship with someone, contract or not. Maybe one day you could look at someone in bed beside you and not be taken aback that they trusted you enough to just . . . sleep right in front of you.

But here it was. Her entire body felt prickly, suddenly; it had grown allergic to being this close to anyone. Maybe this was what everyone else felt, when they woke up next to partners they had chosen for themselves.

She understood now why handlers brought outsiders in for practice. The idea of Ethan being the first man to see her asleep like this made Suyana want to stab something.

(He wasn't, she realized—Daniel had been. That was worse. She set it aside.)

Suyana would have marked Grace as cold as Martine when it came to things like this; even if Grace's politics were in the right place, Suyana felt as if she'd cut herself on Grace's edges whenever they'd talked.

But Grace had changed her mind. Grace was asleep like a child, calm and untroubled. In the late-morning light, her skin was a warm contrast against the white sheets.

The sheets that smelled like hotel detergent.

Suyana shot up with a lurching stomach, remembering what she'd realized just before sleep overtook her.

Someone did the flat's laundry for Grace. Someone else, in the IA's employ, had access to the apartment.

Suyana knew the IA by now. The place was bugged.

She swung out of the bed and up, gingerly testing her right leg before she set weight on it. It held. Grace had rebandaged the wound, and few hours' rest had stopped most of the bleeding. She checked her arm; clean.

That Grace had knelt beside her, wiping blood and wrapping gauze, while she slept helplessly, was something she couldn't imagine. Suyana didn't know how to feel about being trusted. Her skin ached. The backs of her eyes were burning.

She pressed down on the gauze with a shaking hand, but everything held. At least the IA wouldn't have to worry about her bleeding to death before they could find her.

She wished she could take a shower, but she wouldn't be able to re-dress her wounds herself, and there wasn't time. She had to run.

First, there was someone she needed to talk to before she lost her mind doubting.

Her chest tight, she shoved herself into her clothes and approached the viewscreen as if it were a wild animal. If the place was bugged anyway, her secrecy was blown. At least she could get a couple of answers before she hit the streets again.

(There was something disheartening about running without knowing who you were even running from. She didn't mind fighting—she was ready to fight—but she liked knowing who her enemies were.)

Grace's glass of water was sitting on the kitchen counter, one fingerprint turned obligingly outward.

Suyana thought, between one breath and the next, about the wisdom of baiting the animal in its den. Then she picked up the glass by the lip, punched a number she knew by heart, and held the glass against the scanner.

There was a flicker of red light, and Suyana gritted her teeth and waited for the alarm to go off.

But the green light came on. She exhaled shakily as she angled the screen and punched in the keycode to encrypt. There was a beep as the call connected, and before Suyana could rethink bolting, Magnus's face appeared on the screen.

She blinked.

His shirt was rumpled, his tie was gone, his hair was a mess—he must have just run his hands through it to face the strange call ID. He looked like he hadn't slept in a week.

"Samuelsson," he said without looking up, his hands busy with paperwork, his voice polite and disinterested.

She knew that trick; he used it when he wanted to get the upper hand at the start of a negotiation. It worked better when he shaved.

Strange, how much like home it felt to see him. He might be trying to kill her, but there was still something comforting about someone whose tells you knew.

She smiled grimly and faced the screen head-on, to fill the frame with her shoulders.

"Was it you?"

His head snapped up as if it were on a string. His glance went past her for a second—trying to place the location, checking for any shadows that looked like men with guns. To some people, diplomacy came naturally.

Then he was looking at her, frowning but trying not to look as if he'd been caught off balance. "Suyana."

"Was it you?"

His mouth was a thin line. The decoy manuscript was forgotten now; the white curve of it buried the tops of his hands. The paper trembled.

"I don't know what you're talking about."

"I already have two bullet holes in me. No point in being coy now. Was it you."

He flinched when she said "bullet holes."

The papers sank back to the desk. He was distracted, though he'd hardly looked away from her—more like there were too many things he didn't dare say.

Finally he managed, "Are you all right?"

She wished she'd smoothed her hair where it had come

out of place. Maybe then he'd stop looking at her like she was about to keel over. "Still breathing, so far."

"The country's on the verge of real trouble, Suyana. The UARC is not happy with you, and the IA isn't happy with anyone. Do you know they've severed ties with you?"

"*You* severed ties."

"The Committee—"

"Can only lean on those who are willing to break." She was angry, in some vague and distant way. Maybe seeing Colin had reminded her what a handler could be like.

She lowered her head, looked at him through her eyebrows. "If you want me dead I understand, that's how some people leave this job, but don't pretend it was red tape—"

"Goddamn it, Suyana, I didn't want to!"

It stopped her sentence cold.

Magnus never lost his temper. He got cross—he was often frustrated, given how often she and her country stymied his dreams of success—but he simmered and maneuvered, never broke. This was the first time she'd heard real anger from him.

"So why did you?"

"Because I thought it was your best chance," he said. His hands were fists on his desk now, nearly out of frame. "The Committee was extremely unhappy. If I'd held out to try to bring you in, there would have been unpleasantness."

Suyana raised her eyebrows. "I was shot. We've already had unpleasantness."

A ghost of a smile crossed his face. "I forget how good you are about single-minded conversation around the topic you'd like to discuss."

"I forget how good you are at saying things that sound like compliments if you're not actually listening."

He ran his tongue along his teeth. After a moment he said, "I had nothing to do with it. I swear."

She believed him—not because of his promise, but because of his anger. "Do you know who did?"

"No." He sounded wary again. "I'm certainly trying to find out. I was worried whoever it was finished you off after you disappeared from the hospital."

It was an opening for her to tell him who had helped her break out, and explain where she had been. Instead she said, "Guess not."

He bit back a smile.

The list was getting narrower: the Americans, or the IA. Somehow, she didn't see Ethan making that call, but she didn't know very much about his team, and the Americans had never been afraid to spill blood.

"Did you have to explain on the scene?"

Magnus shook his head. "By the time I had my head about me, the Peacekeepers were taking me in for questioning by committee. Just as well. I'll never be able to set foot in that hotel again."

Suyana knew the feeling. "I don't suppose the Americans have been in touch."

"After word first went out, Ethan sent a note expressing his concern and offering assistance. There was no note after the announcement you had been severed."

He was able to say it as if it was a decision he'd never made, a press conference for which he'd never been present. That level of detachment was admirable, in its own way, but goose pimples crawled up her arms.

When he sat forward, the lamplight fell into the circles under his eyes. "Where are you, Suyana? Are you all right?"

"Fine. And I'm surprised you don't know where I am."

"Not for lack of trying," he admitted. "I was worried. At first I thought it might have been some rebellious foolishness, and I ran for the car to tell it not to take you anywhere before I could find out why you'd staged something so dangerous, but as soon as I realized you'd been injured, taken . . ." He trailed off, lifted one shoulder an inch, as much a shrug as he'd ever allow.

His face looked different when he was tired. More honest. She could almost believe he'd been worried about her all this time.

"You'll hear from me soon," she said, "one way or another. Are you prepared to back me?"

He frowned. "What are you planning?"

"You'll know it when it happens." A diplomat's answer; authoritative but without any real facts in it.

"Suyana, who have you fallen in with?"

He was skipping the diplomacy. Impressive. But it was a question with too many answers.

"I'm alone," she said, and even to her own ears it sounded sad enough to be true.

For a moment, he looked at her as if he'd missed her. Then he said, "I've sent an associate to look for you. A private hire. If you keep to the main roads, he'll catch sight of you. When he catches up, tell him he's south of Normandy. He'll tell you they're hardy folk. Then let him know what he or I can do to help. He knows how to reach me. It shouldn't be long."

Suyana supposed that was meant to be reassuring. She smiled a little despite herself, and after a moment he matched it, one eyebrow going up as if he was actually enjoying being on her side.

It would certainly be a novel thing.

Then his expression shifted. She knew this one; this was the face when he wanted to draw the truth out of you before it was too late.

"Suyana. Where are you?"

Downstairs, a car door slammed.

It was nothing—this was Paris, it was daytime, cars were everywhere—but the hair on her neck stood up, and she knew this wasn't a neighbor home early.

She shut the connection.

"How much did you hear?" she asked, without turning.

From behind her, Grace said, "Enough to know you're better at this than he thinks."

Diplomat answer. Still, nothing Suyana had said could have given her away; she wasn't in the habit of confiding.

"I have to go," she said. "They're on their way."

"Who?"

"The IA has your place bugged. Either they actually paid attention to the feed for once, or Colin intervened and gave me up."

Grace looked her flat in the eye and said, in a voice that had nothing of the diplomat in it, "Not from any signal of mine."

"I know," Suyana said, meaning it. "Thank you. But they're still here, and I have to go."

Grace was throwing off the bedding and moving through the apartment, wiping Suyana's water bottle free of prints, sliding a slim stack of euros across the counter. She pointed at her comm bracelet.

Suyana shook her head—it wasn't worth the trouble Grace would be in if they found Suyana carrying it. At this point, they could still claim Grace had been under duress, if they had to. But if Grace had pulled her ID off the bracelet willingly, it put her under the knife too.

Grace said, "Ah, right, the hostage scenario, I see. I'll have a word with Martine, then, in case we need to get a story straight."

Suyana froze. "Is that wise?"

"Don't worry," Grace said. "She's not as bad as she seems. I doubt she could be."

"Do you call on her a lot in crises?"

Grace raised an eyebrow. "You might be surprised."

Suyana really would be. But Grace must know Martine better; maybe Martine just sat around off-camera, brimming with goodwill and waiting to be helpful.

Grace moved to the kitchen and opened a door that Suyana had thought was a pantry. But it was a second set of stairs, narrow and broken-down and filthy, and Suyana could have wept that she wouldn't be fighting her way down as the IA was coming up.

"Take care," Suyana said, nearly under her breath, as she passed.

Grace nodded. "Good luck," she said sincerely, and disappeared from the doorway.

As Suyana caught the landing and pivoted to head down the stairs, the last thing she saw was a sliver of Grace calmly swinging a folding chair, and the conference panel going up in a shower of sparks.

20

Daniel still couldn't quite believe that when Fine Tailoring was recruiting you got a chauffeured car, and as soon as they'd stapled a camera to your temple, you were on the Metro with the rest.

"This seems insulting," he said as he and Bo emerged. "How much do you miss in all that time you spend underground?"

"I don't miss much." Bo was already moving, scanning the street as he went, glancing once at his watch as if he were due to meet Margot for coffee somewhere.

Daniel followed. "What do Kate and Dev do with that footage?"

"What would you do with hours and hours of people on the subway?"

Spy on them for all they were worth. "Nothing."

"Well, there you go."

It was good to know some footage was deleted. It gave him some breathing room, maybe. Somehow. The idea of the rest of his life being on CCTV made the backs of his hands itch and the front of his throat close up.

"This doesn't seem like Margot's kind of neighborhood," Daniel said. "I would have pegged her somewhere more . . . Ritz."

Bo glanced at him for an instant between sweeps of the street. "George V," he admitted.

Of course. What was the point in running the IA if you couldn't sleep in a penthouse suite where your night-light was the glow of the Champs-Élysées?

"So what are we doing this far south of the river, exactly?"

Bo pulled out his phone. "Following a pattern," he said as he dialed. "Keep up, man. Even you must have done some research before you showed up to watch Suyana Sapaki get shot."

"Fuck you," said Daniel politely.

They rounded a corner and headed for what looked like a fortress that time forgot. A tourist sign proclaimed MUSÉE DE CLUNY.

Bo headed around to one of the service doors, where a young man was taking a smoke break that conveniently ended the moment they showed. He left the door open as he went back inside, and Daniel and Bo slipped into the museum.

"Stay one room behind me," Bo said quietly. "You're watching me, not her."

Frankly, he would have watched Bo even if that hadn't been his assignment. Margot was worth spying on, but Daniel knew enough about Margot to guess that if she came here as often as she seemed to, it wasn't to meet anyone. Everyone had one thing they kept just for themselves. If Margot wanted to conduct illicit business, she could do it more easily in the crowds of the Champs-Élysées.

Bo had to know that too. He'd taken the footage. Which meant they were here just because Bo had a favorite.

Daniel intended to catch every look Bo shot her way. Li Zhao looked down on personal involvement between a snap and his target; no telling whether this would be leverage whenever he wanted to graduate to his own beat.

He knew he was being punished for resisting recruitment, but he couldn't help but be a little insulted at the instruction. You didn't get from Free Korea to Europe without being able to blend in.

Bo vanished into the warren of rooms. Daniel picked up

a map from the tourist desk and kept one eye on it as he followed Bo's lazy circle around the ground floor.

Daniel wondered how many field agents Bonnaire Atelier and Fine Tailoring International actually had; how many snaps were walking right now through London, New York, Hong Kong, Cairo. How many in Paris? One of them had to be looking for Suyana now that she was a person of interest.

How much information did they already have about her? Where would they start looking? Had what he'd done only helped them? Was it better for her to be tracked in case someone tried to make her disappear? Would they find her before whoever was after her finished the job?

Eventually Bo stationed himself at the juncture of two exhibits. It took Daniel a second to realize where Margot must be. Bo was good about not quite looking at anything.

Daniel obediently took up a position where he could see them both at a distance, and held his breath.

Margot wore a camel coat and prim heels, her hands clasped around a handbag that seemed too small for the amount of politics she was responsible for. She was standing inside the stained-glass room, bathed in a rainbow of light, her placid face tilted up like a happily receiving saint.

At the back corner, Bo stood against the curve of the wall looking sidelong at the object of his dreams, his body a murky shadow at the head of a hallway full of tombs.

*[ID 35178, Frame 51: IA Committee head Margot standing
in the stained-glass room of the Musée de Cluny, Paris. She is
alone. She does not seem to anticipate a meeting.
Background subject: ID 40291 is recording.]*

By the time Margot left the Cluny it was nearly dusk, and
as they headed out, Daniel said, "There has to be a point at
which crack surveillance teams eat something."

"Only after we're covered by another shift. Margot's
A-level."

Daniel wondered if it was too late to throw himself into
the Seine. "And how did you get this A-level assignment?"

"Li Zhao put me on it a few years back, when the last day
guy got made and had to be relocated in a hurry."

That was only half an answer. "So is Margot under watch
twenty-four/seven?"

Bo gave him an *of course* look. "She's the head of the
Central Committee of the world's biggest diplomatic assembly."

"So why you?"

Bo looked away, let out a heavy breath through his nose.
"We're losing her."

Surprisingly, Margot didn't step into an IA-plated car
to get whisked back to the hotel. Instead, she walked up to
the quay and across the Pont au Double to the Île de la Cité,
looking like a still from an old movie when she turned,

and her profile against Notre-Dame caught the setting sun.

Daniel wondered if this was what would happen to Martine, as photogenic and self-aware as Margot could hope to be, who'd followed Margot's footsteps out of Norway right into the upper echelons of the International Assembly. Martine wouldn't be able to take over anytime soon—Margot wouldn't be giving up that Head of Committee chair until she died in it—but he had a suspicion Martine needed only to reach out with the right gift in hand to be lifted up into the Committee.

Maybe she already had. He'd pay ten grand cash to know whether Martine had given up Suyana. She was a game player. She knew how much that information was worth. It would be all the leverage Martine needed to seal her career.

He wondered if, fifteen years from now, he'd be following Martine down the streets to Terrain the way Bo followed Margot, half hunting and half in love.

They followed Margot at a distance. Daniel kept a steady pace, with Bo catching up with him or falling behind, like two strangers might.

After one pass where Margot glanced toward the river with her hair just beginning to come loose, Daniel said, "She takes a good picture, I'll give you that."

"That's not my concern," Bo said, moving ahead so quickly Daniel couldn't tell what his expression was. "I only care what she's doing."

Even if Bo was better at lying than he was, Daniel would never have believed it. A photographer wanted the best shot, always, no matter what was happening.

Someday, when he could admit it to himself, he suspected he'd look at the photo of Suyana being shot—the sharp line of her profile, the blood in the sunlight, her body not yet coiled to run—and think it was beautiful.

When Margot looked up at the spires of the church, Bo edged through the crowd a few people to his right, to preserve her profile.

Bo hadn't answered Daniel's question about how one got assigned to the most powerful person in the world, but maybe he didn't have to. She was powerful and secretive, even under surveillance. Li Zhao had a knack for this; she'd probably guessed Bo would get too fascinated with Margot to ever look elsewhere.

(Did Bo know it himself? Maybe Bo thought he just liked having a prestige gig. When it was Daniel's turn to follow Martine, would he find himself staring at the curl of her lip every time she delivered an insult?)

The sunset against Notre-Dame was prime tourist material, and the crowd packed tight along the pavers. Margot moved through it like a wisp of smoke, but Bo didn't push forward to follow.

"Aren't you going after her?"

"We'll let this spool out for a while," Bo said, gnawing absently on one corner of his mouth. "No need to risk exposure if she's just here to feel like a spy. If she meets with anyone, I'll move in. You stay here."

If she's just here to feel like a spy. Daniel rolled that one around for a second.

For a few minutes it was just the murmur of the crowd and the honking traffic across the bridge and, every once in a while, a muffled whirring close to Daniel's skull, as his camera transmitted a batch of photos.

Daniel would get used to it. He hoped.

Then a movement through the crowd caught his eye, and Daniel looked up to see the stranger from Bo's last excursion sidling up to Margot.

Bo vanished.

Daniel tried to get a better look without disobeying the order to stay put. He could almost place the man, but who? One of the handlers? Had he been standing in the background of some IA broadcast Daniel half remembered?

The stranger leaned in and said something brief and measured. Daniel couldn't see enough of his expression to draw conclusions.

Then Margot turned.

Her placidity had vanished. Her eyes were narrowed, and her face seemed to pull in on itself and sharpen as she looked him over. The stranger shrank back an inch, which Daniel could only think wasn't far enough.

She said a few words—her voice was diplomat-low, and didn't carry, but from the looks on their faces she was extremely displeased and was explaining exactly what she expected from him, and what he'd be in for if he didn't provide swift and satisfactory customer service.

Bo moved in behind her—far enough back in the crowd that it attracted no attention, but closer than Daniel would have dared. Daniel watched her moving and thought about Kate calling Margot "big game." It seemed an inadequate phrase.

When she was finished, she turned her back without ceremony and walked the bridge back to the north side. Her pace was as calm as when she'd been walking along the quay. She never looked behind her.

Amazing, Daniel thought. Under different circumstances he'd shake her hand.

The stranger stood where he was for a moment, as if gathering his courage. Then he headed in the opposite direction and melted into the crowd. As he turned, his dark hair fell in front of the last sliver of his face.

And—Daniel felt like he'd been cracked across the face—he knew where he'd seen him before.

Daniel had seen the man just for an instant, while half

dragging Suyana toward the avenue, as the man vanished in the chaos after the shooting. He'd been coming around the corner a block from the hotel, heading for Suyana, carrying a thin, dark case across his back.

A case you'd keep a rifle in.

21

Even though she varied her pace, and even stopped to buy a crepe from a sidewalk stand, Suyana made it to the Chordata house in much less time than she'd managed it the day before.

Partly, that was because her wounds were rested and it was slightly less torturous to walk. Partly, it was because she didn't have someone with her whom she was trying to confuse.

She delayed it as long as she could, repeating vocabulary exercises, cycling through languages (she knew six, depending on how much attention she was paying).

The Face has a further comment. The Face wishes to object. The Face accepts the decision of the Assembly. The Face is grateful to the Committee.

She was coming back for the sake of a duty she hated but couldn't shirk, with information they needed. If anyone felt like killing her, they were welcome to take their chances. It would save Chordata the trouble of shooting her when they found out she'd let in a snap.

"Some people you can't trust," Hakan had said. "Some you can. It has nothing to do with what they say here. You learn the difference, with skill and time."

She was sixteen, her first year as the Face of the UARC, watching how politics functioned and trying not to flame out.

("Noqakuna," Hakan told her a lot her first years, tucked into a long sentence in Quechua she understood less and less of. "We," it meant; the version of the pronoun meant to exclude. A sign they were being lied to.)

She could do it, she thought sometimes, as she spoke earnestly to this or that handler who had something she needed; she could do this and thrive. Other times she watched Martine cross the floor like a white bear as the countries around her cringed in their seats, and despaired.

"I think you're just trying to keep me from disappearing," she said.

"Probably," he said, and smiled.

His hair had gone gray at the temples by then. She'd

looked at him and wondered what would happen to her when he gave up his chair at last, and went home.

She'd never found out.

The year Chordata blew up the American offices was a diplomatic disaster: calls no one took and favors that vanished when you called them in, and no answers from home about what they could offer allies.

There were rumors in chambers that no one could have known that outpost was American-owned unless there was a mole in the IA.

Suyana struggled against sanctions, and made impassioned speeches in committee meetings, and finally she'd agreed to make an apologetic PSA as proof the UARC was sorry.

And to make sure the UARC was sorry, someone had made sure Hakan disappeared.

There was nothing said about it, by anyone. She walked into the office one morning and Magnus was waiting, tall and blond, with a face that would always look a little like a stranger's.

He'd been perched on the edge of the desk with a dossier open in his hands, falsely casual, and when he looked up his lips thinned before he said, "Lovely. You must be Suyana."

She'd stood where she was without speaking until he closed the file and said, "I'm Magnus," as if he was giving in by telling her.

He was giving in. She was in shock and in mourning, but she knew how to keep quiet until someone broke.

She rang the Morse pattern on the front bell; when they buzzed her in, she took the stairs deliberately, so Nattereri wouldn't get edgy with whatever weapon he'd brought into the hallway.

He seemed mildly surprised to see her, but she kept her hands visible, and by the time she reached the landing he'd stepped aside to let her through.

Onca slid into sight from the doorway to the bedroom, one arm straight down at her side, holding something Suyana couldn't see—but that wasn't hard to guess.

"I'm alone," Suyana said.

Onca stepped back out of sight for a moment; when she came into the hallway, her hands were empty.

"We're glad you're safe. Where's your friend?"

"He wasn't my friend." The words turned her throat to dust.

Onca looked at her. "Why don't we speak alone," she said finally.

When the bedroom door was closed, Onca turned to her. Suyana noticed she'd toed off her heels, the better to quietly kill an intruder. Onca's eyes were blunt and steady.

"How bad is the news, Lachesis?"

The name was an honorific. It was a pillar that Suyana

could stand against. She was grateful. With the name, it was easier to remember all she had done that might be worthy.

If Chordata killed her now, she'd still have given them what they needed to blow up the American foothold at the edge of the forest. She would still have engineered the "surprise" US port inspection that revealed tankers of waste bound for dumping in the Pacific, where the current would have carried it to their shores. (The IA had passed censure, the first against America in fifty years.)

There would be some things that lived because of her, even if she died. That was good. That was enough. She took a breath.

"He was a snap."

Onca's face sank, the muscles around her mouth going limp, her eyes unfocused as if unable to contemplate the extent of the dangers.

"I didn't know," Suyana said. "I would never have brought him if I had known."

If I had known, she thought, I'd have run the other way as soon as the shooting started, and bled to death first, if that's what it came to.

Onca managed, "How did you find out?"

"I saw the pictures he'd taken of my assassination attempt."

She wanted to call it what it was, to make it clear what she had lived through. Shootings happened when someone had a grudge against you. Assassinations happened when someone needed you out of the way because of what you knew.

If Chordata was going to kill her now for letting Daniel in, she wanted to have everything properly named.

"Were there pictures of us?"

"No. None of this. This wasn't his interest."

"But he knows," said Onca. "Snaps have no honor—he'll tell them everything!"

Suyana thought about how hard he'd gripped her elbow in the moment before he kissed her, his face the expression of a man who doesn't know how to atone for what he's done. His hand was shaking. (She'd known he'd betrayed her, just from that, before the pictures ever came.)

"I came to warn you. You'll need to move this safe house, just in case. And I'll need another contact." Her voice broke, just for a second, as she said, "It's not safe for Zenaida."

Onca's expression was unreadable.

"With respect, Lachesis, this is not a decision I can make. I'll have to discuss this with my commander."

Suyana took a leveling breath.

"Your commander is going to tell you to kill me," she said. "You and I both know."

Onca flinched, but didn't deny it.

"I can't tell you how sorry I am," Suyana said, her stomach

twisting as she spoke. "I've brought this on you, and I know that, but there are greater dangers to both of us than one man who wanted to make a little money on my dating gossip."

She took a step closer to Onca, looked her straight in the eye. "Either the Americans or the International Assembly ordered it, but one or the other wants me dead. Don't do their work for them."

Onca pursed her mouth, cheated one shoulder as if she would turn for the door any second.

"I know what they'll tell you, when you ask," Suyana said. Tears pricked the backs of her eyes, but her voice was steady. "I came here to warn you, knowing what might happen. I want to get back what was taken from me, and if I get it back then I want to do what I believe in, for my country and for you, wherever I can help you. Someone's going to tell you what I've done for you is worthless in light of what's happened. I won't understand it. I want to live. I'd rather fight."

She stopped, took a ragged breath.

Onca looked behind her, running a hand across her mouth and pulling on her bottom lip. It was the gesture of someone trying to make an impossible decision. If Onca reported this, Chordata's response would be clear; she was a liability twice over, and had to be eliminated.

Chordata's tenets were to preserve life no matter their plans—their war was with a system, not security guards—

but the ideal and the reality often ran up against each other. There was no benevolent Chordata central through which sanctions were filtered. They were people; if they thought themselves betrayed, sometimes their mercy faltered.

Suyana focused on breathing in and out.

I could die, she thought, the concept hitting her in a way she hadn't let herself consider on the long walk over as dusk fell. (How could you consider it, and still make that walk?)

In Terrain, there had been the awful danger of discovery, the danger that Martine would get it under her skin to turn Suyana over to the IA and laugh at her foolishness. But a risk wasn't a certainty, and Suyana's cause had been needful, and her allies had outnumbered her enemies. Here, she had no one.

Her hands flexed, and she remembered the moment in Terrain she'd looked at Martine and wondered if the tray she was holding could snap Martine's neck.

(Hakan had always been surprised her diplomacy seemed to come a beat late when she was up against an enemy.

"You're clever enough for this work," he'd say sometimes, at the end of his patience. "The first moment of a confrontation is crucial, and you're always two seconds too late. What are you thinking?"

Suyana had never been able to tell him, "How to get them out of the way.")

Onca looked at the floor, at the ceiling, at the gun that was sitting on the dresser beside the door. Suyana held perfectly still. There was still a water mark on the desk, where Daniel had set his bottle down.

"What will you do if I let you go?" Onca was looking at her now, eye to eye.

Suyana didn't hesitate. "Find him, and settle accounts."

It must have been answer enough. A moment later, Onca opened the door and motioned Suyana through it.

"I have a few hours of work," she said. "I won't have time to worry about this until the morning. I'll get my proof it's been taken care of by then."

Suyana nodded, too relieved to think of what to say. She was already in the doorway before she remembered her good-byes. "I owe you," she said. "I won't forget it."

Onca said, "Good luck, Lachesis."

On the street it was almost night; streetlights were flickering on, storefronts pulling their shutters, brasseries like lanterns.

She struck out south. Daniel would have put himself in the center of the action, so the closer she got to the IA, the better chance she had of running into him.

(Something else told her that, whether he hated her or not, he would be making it his business to know where she was as soon as he could.)

If Magnus had reached his man, he'd be on the move too, trying to reach her.

Whichever one of them reached her first, there would be work to do. If she was going to stand a chance of out-maneuvering the Committee and being reinstated, Suyana needed a corpse.

She was going to get one.

22

Daniel was panicking.

The man was walking in the wrong direction, they were parting ways; Bo would follow Margot wherever she was going, and Daniel would lose the stranger—the stranger he knew, he *knew*, had just been told to finish what he'd started with Suyana.

It was the IA who'd tried to kill her.

Bo had lingered in the crowd to watch Margot cross the bridge. Now he was coming back, nearly at Daniel's side already. Any second, they'd be setting off to watch Margot meet some lesser diplomats and cover her tracks at some restaurant no one sane could afford, and go read quietly at home, waiting for news that this stranger had found Suyana and done the job.

Daniel couldn't breathe. When he turned to keep the stranger in sight, his vision swam.

He spun through his options.

He couldn't take Bo in a fight. He could barely look Bo in the eye; Bo was closing in on six and a half feet in a frame like a cement block.

Daniel could try to slip into the crowd, but the camera would give him away wherever he went, and it would be easy for Dev and Kate to have some field team intercept him. If he broke the camera, there was a chance—

"Park, you awake?"

Daniel blinked at Bo. "Just absorbed in the majesty of the church. Where are we heading?"

But Bo was watching him with the look of a guy who'd woken up to a con.

Don't say we're headed after Margot, Daniel thought. The moment you say that I have to run.

Bo glanced over his shoulder at Margot, who was just visible on the far side of the river. Any second she'd be lost in the crowd. Then he looked back at Daniel.

"Why don't you tell me," he said.

For a second, Daniel was stunned. He probably couldn't trust the offer; Bo was probably just trying to draw him in and then override him. But still. Still.

Daniel was talking as soon as he could draw breath again, tripping over the words. "I know who she talked to—I remember that guy now that I've seen him, I remember him from the hotel, when she—I think he shot Suyana."

Bo raised his eyebrows. "I see."

Daniel steeled himself. Sometimes, either you had courage or you didn't.

"I need to follow this man to make sure nothing's going to happen to Suyana, and if that means we have a problem, then that's what it means."

The man was vanishing—he was almost out of Daniel's periphery, any second he would be gone and Daniel would never find him again.

Daniel took a step back and made fists at his sides.

Bo tilted his head. The world slowed down as Daniel remembered that moment in Terrain when Bo had decided to be frightening. For someone like Bo, that's all it took.

Daniel prepared to run.

Then Bo heaved the sigh of a martyr, pulled out his phone, and set off after the stranger.

It took Daniel two heartbeats to realize what had happened, and another few to catch up; he was quick, but Bo was taller, and trying to gain ground.

"—alley footage," Bo was saying into the phone. "Right. The one Daniel was nosy about—nothing tripped the facial

recognition, Dev, we only had half an inch of his face before. Daniel says this is the same guy, and he got a better look than the camera. If it's not him, I'll murder Daniel and keep you posted. Thanks."

"You think I'm full of shit."

"Very much," Bo said placidly. "You're nothing but an angle."

That hit home.

"Wait," Daniel said anyway (don't take the truth lying down if you can help it), "somehow it's shocking to you I might have wanted to be a snap so I could do all right for myself? Are you in this business for your health? Because—"

"I'm in this business because it keeps me honest."

The words were sharper than Daniel had heard from Bo, and Bo was slowing down, looking at him like someone who wasn't going to allow misinterpretation.

Daniel wondered what Bo had been doing before this; what he had been when Li Zhao found him. It didn't look good that Bo welcomed the idea of being under surveillance because it was safer for him than being left to his own devices.

"Understood," Daniel said finally.

"The thing is," Bo said, "if you're lying, you'll be sorry—you don't want to know what happens if Li Zhao declares you persona non grata. She was IA trained; she knows how to erase problems."

Shit. The Assembly. Daniel pushed back a moment of queasiness. It made sense that those who burn out and never make Face would want to make use of the things they'd been taught, and Assembly handler was a tougher gig than freelance paparazzo. Still, strange to realize how many snakes that place could breed.

With something that might have looked like embarrassment on someone else, Bo shrugged and finished, "And if you're right, I'd be sorry to miss the story, so you've lucked out."

It was a good answer, a fair answer. But Daniel suspected Bo had made an exception in his principles, and that was what it really came down to.

"Who did you lose on a story?"

He regretted it as soon as it was out.

Bo looked at him. Daniel watched his expressions cycle through surprise and confusion and anger, and a long, frightening moment when Bo looked about to confide. But then Bo turned his back and picked up the pace.

Daniel caught up, wondering who Bo hadn't looked out for at the moment he should have.

"You don't engage. You're a journalist, not a knight. Don't get delusions."

"You got it," said Daniel, and the lie sounded so casual Bo didn't even look over.

Now that they were following the stranger, Daniel could

almost breathe again. At least he wouldn't have to wonder what had happened to Suyana; whatever it was, it would play out in front of him, soon.

And whatever she needed, he'd do.

He owed her. He was sorry. He could go the rest of his life and never forget the courtyard of the café as she put her hand out like his shield, in those little hours when she had wanted to believe him.

Kate sent the photos over in a message with the header, "Monsieur Goes to Spy School."

It was odd to look at them. The ID for Daniel's photos was only a number; when the text resolved into focus in the caption he felt for an instant like something was missing.

Made sense, though. Daniel could only imagine what happened if a snap agency got raided by IA troops, and they were able to track you down.

(What if you escaped w.. were just a string of numbers? Were there snaps wandering the world, seeking stories out of habit, taking photos no one ever saw?)

There was nothing in his shots that caught a window, but the footage flipped to the security cameras of the hotel, and the man who ducked out of the building across the way was the stranger from Notre-Dame. The innocuous cant of his shoulders would have given him away to Daniel even if his face hadn't.

"Positive ID," Bo told Kate. Daniel was struck that Bo would so openly admit it, before he remembered that the self-lionizing unlicensed press were better off being honest with each other. He'd been among diplomats too long.

"We'll maintain visual for now, and see how it plays out." There was a beat. "No, no need to send anyone else. Not worth it."

Daniel couldn't tell if that was for his benefit, or because Bo thought he was lying.

Either way, it was just as well. If anything happened now, he'd only have to worry about getting one person out of the way.

For an hour, the stranger walked vaguely northwest.

Occasionally he stopped to chat on the phone, or to look in a shop window; finally, he stopped in a café and ordered an espresso, leaning against the counter and flipping idly through a magazine.

Daniel gritted his teeth. "Any chance he knows and he's baiting us?"

Bo shook his head. "Nobody baiting you is this obvious about it."

They were at the corner of the block. Daniel could just see him in the reflection of the open glass door of the café. Bo had his eye on the back entrance, just in case the guy pulled a runner.

But the stranger didn't have the look of a man who

suspected anything. He looked like a hunter in a blind who was just waiting for his prey to wander past.

Where was Suyana, that this stranger seemed in no hurry to seek her out?

Maybe she'd worked a deal, Daniel thought. That's what diplomats did. Maybe the IA had made her a promise. Maybe she was on her way back in, and Magnus had welcomed her with open arms and didn't know she'd never make it home. Magnus might have made a deal with the IA. Snakes made deals as well as anyone else.

(Daniel hoped, for Magnus's sake, that that wasn't what had happened. He had a feeling Suyana would as soon have Magnus's head as his apology.)

"He's gone," Bo said.

Daniel looked up out of instinct, but the window was empty. "You're kidding."

Bo pulled out his phone, and even a few feet away Daniel could hear Kate laughing.

By the time they were back on his trail fifteen minutes later, Daniel's throat was sour and he felt like his breath was always on the verge of giving out.

Now the stranger had more purpose. Time was somehow running out in a way it hadn't before. He'd gotten sight of what he wanted.

Daniel wondered how much it cost to tap into security cameras along the major roads, and sneak a peek at the feed. He wondered how long it took someone to walk from the Chordata safe house back to this neighborhood.

"He's going to intercept her," Daniel said. "We have to keep up."

They were falling in two blocks behind the stranger, keeping pace. Bo glanced over.

"It's a guess," Daniel said.

"You lie better when you hate the person you're lying to," Bo said.

Daniel wasn't going to argue; he bit back a smile.

Bo picked up the pace—not enough to be alarming, but enough to keep the distance just short of two streets, in case the stranger tried to shake them.

But he was keeping to the main streets, without a care in the world.

(They'd lost him for fifteen minutes. Daniel had the feeling that he'd been off the street cameras because he'd taken a detour to get rid of someone. So long as it wasn't Suyana he didn't care.)

"Park," Bo said, "slow down."

But he couldn't.

The stranger was adjusting something inside his blazer, glancing for an instant over his shoulder at the street, as if gauging how fast he could dodge traffic when he needed to make a break for it. He didn't look behind him. Whatever was about to happen, the stranger wasn't concerned.

Why should he be? Suyana was alone.

"Park," Bo hissed, but Daniel recognized this street— they had skidded across it together yesterday, his hand around her shoulders slipping from the blood, his heart pounding in his ears.

The stranger was heading for the hotel.

He vanished around a corner, but Daniel took a hard left, paralleling him. Now that he knew, it was an easy thing to backtrack, to run down the cobbled alleys and cut him off.

Faster, he thought. Faster, you'll miss it, you'll be too late.

He took a turn so fast that he crashed into the far wall and had to brace himself, shaking his head to clear it, his feet tangling until he could right himself.

Ahead was the restaurant, and behind it the hotel. The little dead end here was too open, and the stranger came into sight before Daniel could think better of it and hide.

Daniel stayed closer to the buildings, but made a beeline not even the stranger could mistake.

The man looked over, frowning for a second, trying to place a face he barely recognized.

(He doesn't know, Daniel thought, he never really saw

me—I was just some kid with his head down who grabbed his quarry out from under him.)

Then something from the other side of the courtyard caught the stranger's eye, and he glanced away.

Daniel followed the stranger's gaze as Suyana moved out from the alley on the far side of the little square and stepped into sight.

Her hair was a mess and she was still wearing what she'd worn to Terrain and the dark circles under her eyes were nearly black, but she was standing under her own power. She looked warily pleased to see the stranger, as if she'd wanted better but would settle for this escort home.

She hadn't moved from the mouth of the alley, and seemed poised to run for it if things went sour. She was cautious, now that she was alone.

Daniel's lungs went tight, and he moved forward before he could even think about the stupidity of what he was doing, getting in front of another bullet.

But he'd made a promise. He owed her.

The stranger, torn between keeping an eye on his target and determining whose side Daniel was on, hesitated a moment—it was all Daniel needed. He doubled his pace.

He'd nearly reached them, when Suyana looked over and saw him.

23

How difficult it was to walk: very. Even with a few hours' rest, she wondered if she'd done too much damage to her leg, and she'd carry a limp with her for a year or two after this was over.

How difficult it was to walk down the center of the wide, lazy boulevards without keeping to the shadows, so that the man who was looking for her could find her: nearly impossible. Once or twice she'd panicked, and had to drop off the avenues and take the warrens of back streets until she could breathe again before heading back to the high roads.

How difficult it was to return to the hotel for their meeting, and be in the shadows of the place where she'd nearly died:

Suyana didn't make it.

She got as far as the restaurant, even as far as slipping in the kitchen door and snagging the first knife she found, just in case. (No one looked up. Brown-skinned, apologetic-looking kitchen staff didn't register here either.)

But she meant to keep going through to the hotel, and her feet just wouldn't go. She stayed in the alley, one cramped block away, while she waited to be found, shivering so hard that her legs could hardly hold her.

How difficult it was to see Daniel again:

She turned to stone.

Her mind tried to parse everything you'd notice about any enemy, if he was gaining on you.

His weapons (no camera, but he was a snap, there had to be one somewhere); his armor (the same coat, stiff at the shoulder with her dried blood if you knew where to look—whatever his new friends had done, they hadn't clothed him); his manner.

And there she stuttered and stopped, because his manner was *terror*.

There were a lot of emotions that could be pretended. Love, annoyance, coldness, complacence; they could be as convincing as the real when applied correctly. More than real. She'd seen all of it. She lived among artists. Daniel was a master of the craft.

If he'd met her any other way, she would have hated him still. She had a knife with his name on it. If he'd appeared with his arms open to embrace her, she'd have killed him.

But there was no mistaking terror. False terror always looked like pantomime. Real terror blew your pupils wide, and made your fingertips stiff, laced your jaw up tight.

(She'd seen terror back home, when police broke up protests; she'd seen it in the mirror the night she spent in prison, when she thought she was going to disappear.)

Daniel was terrified now, and whatever he feared, he was searching for her.

She'd been ready to kill him for what he'd done. Right now, he looked ready to die.

He skidded to a stop in the center of the open square, but his right ankle locked up, and he half crashed to the ground, supporting himself on his arms and scrabbling to get back up.

He hadn't even called her name; he was just looking at her as if he was barely in time. Her stomach sank.

Daniel was twisting as he stood, focused on something else.

She followed his gaze and saw a man (Magnus's man?) moving forward as if time was short and he wanted to get it over with.

The stranger was sliding something back inside his jacket, chest-high.

A gun, she thought. He had a gun. He was planning to use it on her. That was what Daniel knew. Her hands spasmed.

Magnus had told him she'd be easy to find, and so his man had found her, and now he meant to clean up someone's mess, under someone's orders.

(Oh Magnus, she thought, as dizzy as if she'd been struck in the temple. Not you. Please not you.)

She breathed in—how long had she been holding her breath? How many seconds had passed while she was trapped in her body?—and saw that it was too late for her to run. The stranger was bearing down on Daniel.

The two of them were swallowed in a blur of motion; Daniel was swinging the stranger off balance, yanking at his jacket, the stranger's fists flying.

Then she heard the crack of an elbow against a skull, and Daniel made one sickening whimper before he dropped like a stone.

Suyana's mouth went dry.

The stranger stood up and stepped out of the puddle of what had been Daniel.

"He was going to kill you," the stranger said.

His voice was flat, purged of whatever accent he'd started with, and overlaid with one that sounded like he'd made it up to avoid where he'd started from.

"Was he?" said Suyana. Her voice was steady. "Thank God you got here in time."

The man was moving around Daniel's body (Daniel's body, Daniel's body, no), extending his right hand to shake with her. His gun hand.

Magnus should have hired someone better for his dirty work, she thought. She gritted her teeth to keep her expression neutral as they shook hands as pleasantly as any two people who weren't carrying a knife and a gun.

Before she could mention Normandy, he said, "There's a room waiting at the hotel where you can get cleaned up before we talk about what's next. Magnus set it up for you, he'll meet us there."

No, she thought. No; to her bones.

She'd stood in Grace's flat, watching ghosts move across Magnus's face. Magnus would never set foot in that hotel again, he'd said, and meant it.

Magnus would have told as much to any man he'd actually hired; this stranger wasn't one of them. This stranger was just trying to get her somewhere he could kill her quietly and pin it on whoever needed something pinned on them.

(It wasn't Magnus. There was a flicker of relief that kept her from tipping into panic. This man wasn't working for Magnus.)

"Very thoughtful," she said, smiled a little, just politeness. "I'd love a bath."

She stepped aside and indicated the alleyway as if it were a grand foyer. She could just see Daniel's body in her periphery, sprawled and still on the stones.

The knife blade pressed against the small of her back as she moved.

She could hardly hear anything over the sound of saliva as she swallowed, and the tips of her fingers were going numb, but it was the smallest of her worries.

She was ready to do what she had to do.

(It was the first thing she always thought: how to get them out of the way.)

The stranger moved as if to walk ahead of her, but as he passed he grabbed her left wrist, twisted, pulled. It mangled the wound on her arm, and she hissed as he yanked her toward him, staggering two steps into striking range. He can't see the knife, she thought. If he sees the knife, this is over.

It overwhelmed her.

She threw her head back as hard as she could.

He was quick—she only caught him on the jaw, not the nose—but still he grunted with pain and swung her a little out of range as he turned her to face him.

They were already halfway down the alley, and now he was blocking the way back to Daniel, but it was an open shot to the hotel behind her.

Which meant he couldn't see that Daniel was struggling

to prop himself up on one elbow, that Daniel had something in his outstretched hand.

"I hope I was worth a lot of money," she said, "for all the trouble you've gone to."

The stranger's mouth pinched thin—it was the only indicator she'd seen that he had any opinions about his work; this was a professional duty. There was no grandstanding here.

"I'll make it quick," he said, reaching into his jacket for the gun.

Daniel threw a stone.

His hand was shaking, he didn't have any balance, it was a miss from the moment it was out of his fingers—but the stranger couldn't see that, and at the sound of the rock hitting the wall he froze for a second, just reflex.

For an instant, his attention faltered.

She locked her left leg to gain an inch of traction, reached behind her with her free hand for the knife, and brought it up between them as hard as she could.

The blade connected with something, sank into warm clay with a wet, sickening sound, driving up and up until it crunched against rock and lodged there.

For a heartbeat, nothing happened.

Then the stranger's weight sank forward onto her.

She sucked in a horrified breath, twisted aside so he wouldn't crush her. Then, between one step and the next, as he fought for equilibrium, she bore forward as hard as she could, so close to him that the end of the hilt pinched against her sternum. The smell of blood was everywhere.

I'm going to be sick, she thought, and then for a terrible moment, We're going to fall together.

But it was enough to push him free of her. With the knife still in his chest, he took two or three shaky steps. On the fourth he faltered; at the mouth of the alley, he fell. He was gasping for breath. Red froth filled his open mouth. Suyana pressed her lips against bile; she wasn't sorry and wasn't sorry and wasn't sorry.

At last, his head dropped back, and he was still.

Someone was calling her name, from far away, but Suyana was walking forward as if in a dream. She stepped over his outstretched arm and into the square, so when she looked at him his face was upside down.

There was a bruise forming along his jaw, where she'd struck him. Blood was pooling everywhere. The hilt of the knife was covered.

When she looked down, her hands were covered in blood—on the left from her wound, on the right from his. She brushed them absently, one against the other.

She was cold, maybe. Maybe she was just standing in shadow, that was all.

Had this been what the assassin had felt three days ago, when he propped his rifle on the windowsill and prepared to fire?

"Suyana. Suyana."

Someone was touching her shoulder, gently, as if they knew she was wounded. She looked up, slowly, from the body.

It was Daniel. Half his face was swollen and already turning blue. When he saw her expression, he flinched and brought a hand to his temple, but on the opposite side, covering a little dark spot that looked like a freckle.

Somehow, that broke the shock—that little gesture that gave him away.

It was a camera.

That was how snaps got the footage they got. Their whole bodies were cameras, and their every waking moment was a spy. He'd covered it so no one could see her.

Her chest felt like it would crack open.

He didn't say anything. He was looking at her with an expression she'd never seen from him. Not even the moment before the kiss had looked like this.

He looked alone.

Finally he said, "Is any of the blood yours?"

"Some. Is it still recording sound?"

"I don't care. Are you all right?"

"You came back to warn me?"

Daniel tried to smile. "Nah, I came back for my camera."

The words scratched his throat, and his breath faltered in the middle. She watched him for a second.

"Hand me the gun," she said.

She wiped it absently on the hem of her shirt, and set it near the outstretched fingers of the corpse. It should be in his hand if it was really going to be convincing, but she couldn't bear to touch his fingers, and this would fool who it needed to fool.

"He killed Magnus's man before he got here," she said as she stood. "Whose man was he?"

"Margot's."

She looked at him, went cold down to her toes.

Margot, the head of the IA Committee that had burned her out three days ahead of protocol. Margot, who must know something she shouldn't.

"Was it . . . just her?" Her voice sounded like she'd swallowed sand.

Daniel shrugged. "I hope so."

He didn't have to say, *Because otherwise, the whole IA wants you dead.*

Suyana had stood up for Chordata a long time ago; Margot wasn't the kind of diplomat who forgot a thing like that. Margot didn't let problems linger. Had she found proof of Chordata somewhere, or had she just gotten tired of waiting for any, and just wanted to plug a leak?

Well, Suyana thought, her insides knotting tight. They could try again to kill her, if they wanted to take their chances, but she was going to crawl out of this, and higher.

"I have to go," Daniel said.

Right, she thought. Of course. He's leaving. Of course. Out of habit, she nodded as if it made sense.

She wanted to thank him; she wanted to forgive him the way he looked like he needed to be forgiven. She opened her mouth.

But someone was moving out into the center of the square (another snap, she guessed—the light was better from the far angle) and they were out of time.

She rested her hand on his shoulder, just for a second, where he'd kept her from falling on that first long run. There was someone else's blood on her hand, but it didn't matter. Everything else about them had started in blood; forgiveness could too.

He covered her hand with his, a heavy pressure on her knuckles.

He said, "Look for me."

It wasn't much of a farewell—it was a warning—but still she pressed the flat of her hand to his coat as if she could reach his heartbeat.

He'd been a traitor, but he'd come back to warn her.

(She'd woken in the bed in Montmartre and seen him standing guard at the door, and something in her heart had turned over. She'd needed a friend, then. She still did.)

She leaned in, close enough that the sound wouldn't carry to the camera, breathed, "I'll see you."

His hand tightened around hers. Then he was gone, vanishing between breaths, and the next time she saw him he'd be a stranger.

She stood where she was, after Daniel had gone. She didn't look over at the shadows of the opposite building where the gentleman from Terrain was standing, trying not to be seen. From there, he had the best shot of her standing over the body of the man who'd tried to kill her; her hair and eyes were wild, her face scratched, one leg was shaking and ready to buckle, and her hands were smeared with blood.

Her mind whirred.

When the IA got hold of this, she'd tell them how the man who tried to shoot her had dragged her away from the hospital—had vanished with her and blindfolded her in a room she never saw, threatening to kill her in retaliation for the formation of the UARC.

(It was a safe threat for the IA; a madman's threat, a thirty-year-old grudge, a goal that would galvanize national pride. It kept the threats from sounding personal.

There would be no personal threats. She wouldn't invent physical harms where there had been none, not even for tele-vision.)

He'd have brought her back to kill her in front of the hotel where she was meeting the boy she loved, the American boy, in secret. He'd have hated her freedom of choice, in picking a boy so far above her station.

The Americans would honor their relationship contract after that. The public would give them no choice.

Magnus would never breathe a word about it; no diplomat would dare look so taken in.

Margot was a different story. Facing down Margot would have to wait until Suyana was too big to disappear. Until then, Suyana would be careful not to suggest anyone from within the IA could have known a thing. Margot had seen her as a threat just for disobeying once, and had guessed close to the mark when she'd called for Suyana to disappear; Suyana had to be careful to be too famous for even Margot to dare.

The stranger's eyes were glassy, by now, and his fingertips stiff and turning waxen.

She wanted to be colder than this, and crueler. She tried to imagine Martine slicing someone's throat one-handed without spilling her drink. But it didn't help, just now; a man was dead, and she had done it.

It's just as well, she thought, numbness spreading through her. I needed a corpse.

Behind her was a rush of sound, as the first IA press photographers arrived.

24

In the upstairs offices of Bonnaire Atelier, Daniel sat with Bo and Dev and Kate and Li Zhao and watched the evening news.

It was the American channel, because their first few hyperbolic minutes on a topic were usually the best way to gauge how the story was going to be shaped for consumption by other nations.

Someone's shaky camera footage of Suyana standing over the stranger's body was playing with the volume too high—the sound of shutters clicking flooded out the audio. Reporters were calling to her in French, in Mandarin, in German.

"What happened? Ms. Sapaki? Ms. Sapaki, what happened?" the cameraman was asking her in English, panning back and forth from the corpse to her face.

Suyana looked at him, blinked slowly.

You'd think she was still in shock, if you didn't know what to look for, if you didn't see her eyes drop for half a second to some national credentials he was wearing that pleased her.

She shook her head. "He would have killed me," she said, sounding unbearably sad.

That was real. That voice Daniel remembered, when she'd looked down at the man she'd killed.

He wished he'd stayed long enough to tell her not to be sorry. It wouldn't have worked, but still, it wasn't as if he would get another chance to tell her.

The camera panned down to her bloody hands. Before it could snap back to her face for a reaction shot, her voice came over the video: "I just want to go home."

"Voice-over," cut in Dev. "They looped that later. Cheating."

"Nope," said Kate, her head tilted like she was playing it back internally and watching for the seam. "Background noises match up. Real audio, poor camerawork."

Dev shook his head. "No way. Face or not, no one gives a quote like that standing over a corpse!"

"You should meet her sometime," said Bo.

The video froze after the pan from her bloody hands to

her anguished face (how could you top that?), and shrank to the screen behind two breathless anchors.

"Delegate Sapaki is currently resting comfortably at her Paris quarters after receiving medical attention," said the first anchor, "and is reportedly recovering from her injuries."

"A lucky break for her," said the second anchor.

Daniel ran his tongue over his teeth.

The first anchor nodded solemnly. "The reasons for Sapaki's assassination attempt and abduction have not been confirmed, though there are reports it was at least partially in retaliation for her secret relationship with American delegate Ethan Chambers."

Everyone in the room pointedly didn't look at Daniel. He didn't know why. He'd known that before he'd started taking pictures.

The second anchor was taking up the cause. "According to the United Amazonian Rainforest Confederation handler, Magnus Samuelsson, Sapaki is scheduled to make a public statement about the incident tomorrow morning in the General Assembly. You'll be able to watch it live at eight, right here—"

Li Zhao hit a button, and the screen went blessedly black.

"If I had the full footage of this fight," she said, "we'd all be millionaires."

Daniel's heart seized.

Kate's face went very still. "Why don't we have it?"

"Because Bo arrived only moments before the first IA press got there. And Daniel's camera seems to have malfunctioned due to impact, so there's no alternate footage to fall back on."

Daniel forced himself not to look around—Li Zhao would be looking for signs of guilt—but in his periphery, Bo and Dev exchanged quick glances.

So, footage could be kept off the servers. Footage could be erased if someone in the basement was on your side. That little shit Bo never told me, he thought, and bit back a smile, fought the urge to take a big, free breath.

"However," Li Zhao went on, her eyes lighting on each one of them in turn, "we do still have that few seconds of this filleted gentleman dropping into the alley and Suyana Sapaki making sure he knew who killed him before he shuffled off this mortal coil. There are currently seven magazines and three governments bidding on the footage, and more offers coming in, though some of them seem to be under the impression that we run a charity, so we'll be concentrating on offers that aren't insultingly low."

"Are any of them the UARC?" Daniel didn't know why he'd asked. Li Zhao looked at him. Then she stood.

"Daniel, in my office, please. The rest of you, good night."

Inside, she sat behind the desk without any indication

what he was meant to do. Daniel wasn't sure if this was a test or just office procedure, so there was a ten-second delay before he took his seat.

She rested her laced hands on the edge of the desk.

"I don't want you to walk out of this room thinking you got away with anything," she said.

Her voice was calm and cold, and Daniel held his breath.

"The specifics have, in fact, been wiped off the servers, thanks to what I'm sure is a software malfunction that will never happen again. However, diagnostics confirmed that even after you hurled yourself in front of a bullet to save Suyana—I'm just guessing—your camera was recording."

"How strange," said Daniel, after all other excuses had escaped him.

"Indeed." She sat a little forward in her chair, her desk lamp casting shadows over her hands as she clicked through something on the computer. Daniel saw quick flashes across the glare in her glasses—some photos he probably didn't want to look at.

"And after serious thought, in order to forestall any further malfunctions, you've been reassigned. Bo made a recommendation given your demonstrated capabilities in the field, and I agreed because I suspect your new assignment will actually keep you where I ask." She sat back, crossed her arms over her chest.

Daniel didn't like the sound of that. He narrowed his eyes. "Aren't you afraid I'll pull a runner just to test your conclusions?"

It came out sharper than he meant, and she blinked once before her mouth curved into a thin, dangerous smile.

"Oh, please," she said. "Try me."

His breath caught in his throat. After a second, he forced a grin. "Tell me the assignment, then, and I'll tell you if it's good enough to keep me."

Li Zhao looked him in the eye, and Daniel suddenly felt slightly dizzy, without knowing why, for the heartbeat before she said, "Suyana Sapaki."

When he came onto the landing outside the flat, Kate was waiting for him, leaning against the banister with a look that worried him.

"Weird glitch on your camera," she said.

"It was a crazy few minutes."

"I'll take your word for it."

He half smiled, headed for the stairs.

"Not a lot of blackouts on my feed," Kate said.

He stopped, looked at her. In this light, the tips of her hair looked like the spark point at the base of something burning.

Quietly, he said, "What is this about?"

"This system isn't one I like gaming," Kate said. "We

have a bad enough reputation without playing card tricks on one another."

He felt like Kate was also the kind to spy on the subway footage for all it was worth.

"Bo was the one who came late to the scene," he said. "Take it up with him."

Kate's eyes narrowed. She shifted her weight, flexed her fingers around her cane; the leg braces glinted. "Did Bo tell you what he did before he became one of us?"

He forced a shrug. "Nope."

(He didn't know how Suyana lived under this kind of dread; the dread of waiting for someone to say something you already feared.)

"Hired gun," Kate said. "Maybe you want to think about how likely it is that he'd miss any of that."

The dread settled.

Daniel remembered what Bo had told him about staying honest, just before they gave up on Margot and crossed the bridge after the stranger. He thought about Bo biding his time around the corner in the alley, listening to a hired gun being killed, and waiting for the moment it was safe to record. Daniel wondered what Bo had done, just before he came to Fine Tailoring, that needed a permanent camera making him accountable in order to make amends. Not that Daniel had a lot to say about that, today.

(Daniel stopped wondering why Li Zhao had assigned Bo to follow Margot. He knew what Margot was capable of. Bo was the most likely to survive it.)

"And what did you do before you landed this fantastic gig?"

"Nothing. I was with Li Zhao so early I helped her change her name."

He did some math about how old Kate was, knowing Li Zhao had been in the IA once, and wondered which high school class Li Zhao had managed to pull Kate out of, and what exactly Li Zhao had done wrong in the IA, that she slid into this industry like a knife.

"Of course," he said, and it sounded so flat she smiled a little more kindly, just for a second.

"I try not to have enemies here. I like us to be better than the people we follow. But there aren't a lot of tech glitches on my watch."

Daniel slid his fists into his pockets.

"Noted," he said.

(He missed Suyana, just for a moment, like he'd pulled at an old wound.)

When Kate tilted her head and smiled, her silver earrings caught the moonlight. "Have a great night, Daniel."

Outside on the street, he fought the urge to look behind him. No one would be following him.

They didn't need to. He spied on himself.

*[ID 40291, Frame 146: Suyana Sapaki standing
outside the front court of Hotel Sinople. She stands
over the corpse of an unidentified male, who has a
knife wound. The hilt of the knife remains lodged in
the sternum. Sapaki's hands are bloody. She looks into
middle space.
Preceding circumstances unknown—see also note on
frames 108–145.]*

[ID 40291, Frames 108–145: Blackout.]

Daniel had waited on the broad avenue for a long time.

He watched the first flush of IA photographers come
barreling down the avenue and turn just before they reached
him, their hands already on their cameras.

(Bo must have made the tip-off call to the officials by
then. Smart move. The footage Bo had already taken would
be worth eight times as much if the story broke wide open
and people were clamoring for the dirt.)

Still, Daniel couldn't bring himself to go back the way he
had come and film Suyana standing over the body of the man
who had almost killed her.

The IA press gave way to the local news, and finally to an
armored van and a trio of chauffeured cars with the two-dove
crest of the IA. Peacekeepers poured out of the van on their

way to secure the scene; the men and women in dark suits didn't deign to get out of their sedans.

Except one. Magnus leaped out of his car before it had even fully stopped, moving so fast he nearly overtook the Peacekeepers on his way down to the alley.

Good, Daniel thought.

A few moments later, Bo was back on the avenue.

"Peacekeepers spoil the party?"

"We did what we could," Bo said. "You can't always catch everything." (Daniel didn't know what Bo was telling him—not then.)

"Thanks," Daniel said, cleared his throat, and wondered how he could possibly go on.

Bo shook his head. "Let's get back," he said. "Li Zhao will want to dissect the news and start packaging the footage."

A crowd of gawkers was already gathering behind the Peacekeeper tape, and police lights flickered off the buildings down the street. It was easy to disappear into the thick of it, walk at no great speed until you were well away from prying eyes.

When they were halfway to Bonnaire Atelier and Fine Tailoring, Bo looked down at him.

"What made you see her as a mark?"

There were easy answers. She'd been in a PSA on American TV after the terrorist thing; she'd been in a charity fashion spread in French *Vogue* last year—a group shot, in the back line. They were good indicators that a Face's barometer was slowly rising. If you'd been following it long enough, you could put money on those. (Some did; there was a decent trade in off track Face futures.)

"I saw a portrait of her in some magazine a couple of years ago. In an awful dress, Magnus next to her. And she was smiling, but her fingers were digging into the bottom of the desk like it was about to fall apart. I didn't think much about it for a long time, but I remembered it."

Bo hadn't answered; they walked in silence for a long time, as Bo looked like he was trying to make up his mind about something.

At the threshold of Fine Tailoring, he said, "That's good to know."

But that was all he said, and then it was time to go inside, where Kate and Dev were cataloging their photos and Li Zhao was looking them over, and then everyone would gather to watch the evening news.

The public gallery of the IA's General Assembly Français was a mezzanine crescent above the round chamber, behind a plate of bulletproof glass.

Daniel had learned, among other things, that headset rentals were ten euros, and guaranteed pickup only for the mikes at the head stage; if you happened to catch the murmurs of the floor, it was serendipity.

He'd also learned that whatever his camera was made of didn't trip metal detectors or tech wands, though he couldn't help thinking someone could have spared him that moment of panic.

The crowd was most dense near the center, where you could see the featured speaker head-on, but Daniel had watched more of these proceedings than most, and knew the place to get prime photos was in the wings.

As stagehands and techies scrambled back and forth doing sound tests, Daniel took up a place as far left as he could get, so he had a clear vantage stage right. That seemed to be where the channel of action was.

Delegates and their handlers filed in from the three doors that surrounded the lower level. Daniel recognized Grace and Martine at the first row of tables, closest to the cameras, where the Big Nine sat.

Coming in close behind them was Ethan Chambers, who at least had the decency to look concerned and romantic as he took his seat.

(One of the other snaps had come back to Fine Tailoring with news that he'd seen signed papers being transported from the American office.

"I wanted you to know," Kate told him from behind her

monitor. Her eyes slid to his; she'd meant it as a kindness. Not that it felt that way, but it was the thought that counted.)

He wondered if anyone had been glad to see Suyana come back to the fold. Maybe some of them were her friends. Daniel hoped so. Suyana should have someone she could trust.

He didn't dare think, *Me*. Everything about him was a spy. He wondered if Li Zhao had known it would be worse like this, always looking but afraid to ever find her.

But he wouldn't let it turn into a punishment. It stung, and it would always sting, but it was better than not knowing about her. Anything was better than not knowing.

The Central Committee filed in last. Most of them took the stairs to the side of the stage and found a place in the risers of upholstered chairs grouped stage left for them; just ostentatious enough to be seen, just far enough to seem out of the way.

Margot kept walking right to the center of the stage. She was wearing a pale-blue suit a shade lighter than her eyes, and her face was a mask of noble altruism.

She delivered her introduction smoothly, took her seat at the front of the Committee, without a care in the world.

Daniel never heard what she said. He was already leaning against the glass, looking for Suyana as she cleared the wings.

She wore a turquoise dress that made her look older and sharper than he'd ever seen her, and her long hair swung like a pendulum as she crossed the stage.

The look she gave Margot was that of two people at war, and Daniel had two thoughts at once—*Be careful*, and *What a story that will be.*

He tried not to feel guilty. There was no harm in it, now. That was just what he was.

The angry, ugly bullet wound on her arm was Suyana's only jewelry, and it burned purple and white against her skin under the lights all the way up to the podium.

She took her position, her hands curled around the sides as if she were bracing for impact. She cast an eye around the room—Daniel thought her eyes lingered as she looked across the Big Nine, but maybe that was just something the Big Nine required.

Then she scanned the gallery.

There was no way to prove she'd seen him. Her eyes flickered past the rows in turn, and then she was looking away, and even the camera couldn't say she had looked him in the eye. But she had. Just for an instant, she'd looked right at him. His hands were heavy; his lungs pulled tight.

(Once—it seemed very long ago—he'd looked at her and thought that following her was the luckiest thing he'd ever done.)

He held his breath for what felt like minutes, watching the lines of her face.

The camera took a thousand pictures as he watched her. It was a sound he was already used to; he hardly heard it anymore.

[*ID 35178, Frames 204–208: Suyana Sapaki facing the floor of the IA, beginning to speak.*]

[Classified] (For tomorrow —M)

6:30 a.m.	Breakfast with UARC Vice President (His car to pick you up outside hotel) [Cameras expected]
7:30 a.m.	Interview, *Closer* magazine, home hotel suite
8:00 a.m.	Breakfast with Ethan Chambers (F-USA), Café d'Hiver [Cameras expected]
9:00 a.m.	UARC local news briefing [Suyana, Magnus]
9:30 a.m.	Breakfast Event: "Brighter Tomorrow Victims' Services" (Keynote speech attached)
10:30 a.m.	Roll call in chambers
11:00 a.m.	Hear motions presented [Cameras expected]
11:30 a.m.	Lunch with Grace Charles (F-UK), George V [Cameras Expected]
12:30 p.m.	Global news briefing [Suyana, Magnus]
1:00 p.m.	Lunch with South American Committee, Café Rio (Car service confirmed) [Cameras expected]
2:00 p.m.	Committee Meeting, Cultural Heritage International
3:00 p.m.	Car service to photo shoot
3:30 p.m.	Photo shoot, *Closer* magazine
5:30 p.m.	Car service from photo shoot
6:00 p.m.	Stylist call for evening events
6:30 p.m.	Dress for cocktail event
7:00 p.m.	~~Cocktail Event: Olympic Committee Reception,~~ ~~LA event space [Cameras expected]~~ Global and local news briefing [Suyana, Magnus]
7:30 p.m.	Cocktail event —SS
8:00 p.m.	Dress for dinner event (Car service confirmed)
8:30 p.m.	Dinner with Ethan Chambers, Restaurant David Alain [Cameras expected]
10:30 p.m.	Car service to red carpet event
11:00 p.m.	Red carpet event, Diamonds of Hope fund-raiser [Cameras expected]
12:00 a.m.	Evening event, Terrain [Privacy requested]
3:00 a.m.	End of day

25

Suyana gave herself a gift, and forgot some things.

It didn't matter what happened after Magnus appeared and asked the IA press for "please no more questions," and pretended he'd never seen the corpse under her feet.

She could forget how it felt when Magnus took her shoulders harder than he had to, told the cameras she had no further comment at this time, kept her at an angle as they walked so he could look into her face.

(No knowing what he'd found. Better not to ask.)

She could forget the walk to the car—she'd had to step over the body's outstretched arm, which would have been terrible, if she remembered it—could forget how her body had turned to stone when she saw the ambulance and she'd insisted no hospitals; she forgot that Magnus took her in his car instead, cleaning the blood from her hands with some wipes he'd charmed off the medics, so that when she arrived at the hotel they would let her inside without making a scene.

She could forget the photographers outside the Pierrot, and however she must have looked to the cameras as she walked past them. She could forget the bouquet of flowers the concierge delivered, with compliments of Ethan, who wished to be informed of anything he could do.

There were problems she'd have to face in the morning, but she'd stood over a corpse and played the part that had to be played, and the rest would wait for her. She could forget some things.

She closed her eyes; she dreamed of the forest.

Her first visitor was Magnus, who came with the doctor just before dawn so she could be pronounced well enough not to faint on television.

"Thank you so much for your attentions," Magnus said as he escorted the doctor to the door. "The Assembly makes excellent recommendations, we couldn't be happier with your work. Will there be serious scarring, do you think?"

"Yes," the doctor said. "I don't know how badly, but there

was a lack of sufficient treatment after the initial injury, and she's been hard on herself."

"Of course," Magnus said, which meant, *That's a shame*; then he thanked the doctor handsomely for his time, and closed the door.

When he came back into sight in the entry hall to her bedroom, he leaned against the door frame and came no farther. His hands were in his pockets, and his eyes fixed on the foot of the bed.

"You didn't say, last night, what happened."

There was no blame in his voice for what she'd done. It was more generous of him than she'd expected, for him to trust her reasons.

She considered what she knew he could find out, balanced against secrets she might be able to keep. If he knew Margot was against her, he might help; there were alliances that could be made, and Magnus was a master of the game.

But if he knew, he could also turn her over to Margot, if things ever soured at home. Margot wanted a lot of people gone. Suyana couldn't risk that Magnus would ever be willing to hand her over for a chance at Margot's good graces. It was no good telling Magnus too much of the truth.

"He was going to kill me," she said, settling on the cleanest lie. "He killed your man, I guess."

Magnus started to look at her, stopped. "Yes."

(Some things she hadn't forgotten. There were things she knew about the way a blade cut through the body that would never go.)

Then she said, "It was a good lesson. We've both learned something."

He frowned. "Suyana—"

"I should shower and dress," she said. "If you'll excuse me."

And because he was a diplomat, and manners must trump pride, he closed the door behind him without another word.

Her second visitor was Grace, who arrived just as the suite phone started ringing.

Magnus let her in, looking a little surprised that they rated a visitor from the Big Nine, and then headed straight for the phone.

"Sorry," said Grace. "It's probably our fault the press figures you're awake."

"'Our'?"

Grace rolled her eyes. "Colin insisted on coming. He's hovering in the hallway just in case one of the porters pulls a gun."

Suyana smiled, and indicated the pair of chairs farthest from Magnus.

Magnus was already handling the call, his fingers flying over his tablet. "No interviews until after the press conference," he was saying. "I'm sure you understand, but after that we can of course look at her schedule—"

"How did your evening go, with the excitement? Was Magnus your last dance?"

Grace's posture was the picture of ease; you'd never know she was asking if the man ten feet away had tried to kill her.

"No," Suyana said. "My guest from Terrain helped me sort out my dance card."

"I see. Do I want to know?"

"It's worth your life," Suyana said.

After a moment, Grace shook her head.

"The United Kingdom wishes to extend its warmest sympathies," she said instead, in her public voice. "It admires the UARC for its determination and its victory, and looks forward to working together on committee projects to which, I understand, you'll soon be invited."

Grace's rueful smile started about halfway through her speech, and Suyana had to bite back a grin.

"The United Amazonian Rainforest Confederation thanks the United Kingdom for its kind words," Suyana said, pulling a face Magnus couldn't see. "I look forward to further negotiations of our countries' best policies."

Grace tilted her head to hide her smile from Magnus. "Very kind," she said, as the bell rang, and Martine let herself in.

"Christ," she said, "I got up in the dark to come down

here before the photographers could roll out of their pens, and I still end up walking a gauntlet. What exactly do they think they're going to get a shot of, milling in front of the hotel, you murdering a waiter? Hello, Magnus. Grace."

She sat without invitation on the third seat.

Magnus seemed too baffled by her presence to have taken offense, and before he could decide whether to mention it, the phone rang again, and he was off to the races.

Suyana took great offense to pretty much everything about Martine, but didn't think it was worth provoking someone who had kept quiet about the first secret she'd been handed.

"Martine," she said. "The United Amazonian Rainforest Confederation welcomes you."

"The Kingdom of Norway had better damn well be welcome at this hour," Martine said. She slid a small pastry box across the coffee table between them. "The Honorable Ambassadorship of Too Shy to Show Her Face hopes you're recovering well from nearly being shot to death."

"Martine, really."

"Very well, thank you," Suyana said. Then, feeling a little wicked, "It was a long way to come to deliver this, though. The George V has to be five, ten blocks from here."

"I wanted to see how mean you looked before the stylists got you made up," Martine said. "It's been worth the trip."

"We'll leave you," Grace said, standing and shooting Martine a look that left no room for negotiation. "We know you'll have a very busy day, and I'm sure you'll want to prepare for Ethan, when he arrives."

"Ethan?" Suyana blinked.

Martine huffed a laugh. "You said something to the cameras about how much you'd missed him in captivity. Either you're really in love with the shallowest boy in the IA, or you're an artist."

Suyana was grateful for the warning. Ethan would bring cameras with him. Magnus needed to call a stylist, now.

"Good luck today," Grace said.

"Thank you," said Suyana. She was already opening the little bakery box with two tiny cakes inside. They were frosted white; one was topped with a candied violet, one with a blue fondant bird.

Gooseflesh crawled up her arms.

(She would have a contact soon. The message was signed in violet and stamped with Kipa's Passerine; this message had come from their mutual friends. And she was telling Suyana, because Chordata had told her it would be all right. It felt like she could breathe, suddenly.)

"Don't eat those," said Martine.

Grace was nearly at the door, waving her good-byes to Magnus, but Martine was still standing over her.

"Why not," Suyana guessed, "they'll ruin my matronly figure?"

But Martine was looking right at her, and the archness in her face was gone. "Because from now on, you don't know what's poisoned. You've been smart. Don't die before nightfall, if you can help it."

Long after the door had closed behind them, Suyana sat and stared at the pair of cakes.

Martine was right. Not about these—though Martine was a courier of dubious merit, she wasn't a poisoner.

But Margot wasn't going to stop at one chance, and she wouldn't risk making Suyana a martyr again. When the next turn came, it would be something that looked like an accident.

Still, there was a flicker of joy inside her, looking at them, the violet and the blue bird side by side.

The feeling lasted until she remembered the photographers outside; they'd be outside today, and tomorrow, and if she was lucky, she would continue to be important enough to be documented.

It would be nearly impossible to move under the radar, as she had before.

Now she'd have to work to create a Suyana Sapaki for the IA and the public who wouldn't think of such a thing, a Suyana Sapaki so separated from the idea of revolution in the minds of the IA that not even a breath of Lachesis would ever reach them.

"Suyana?" Magnus was kneeling beside her, his face a mask of worry. "You look ill."

"We need to call a stylist," she said.

Oona was one of the general-purpose IA stylists, assigned to the lesser countries for the rare times they were called on to make an appearance and say something they were supposed to say.

"So," she said, scrolling through her tablet. "There's a press conference? I can get you animal print, if you want, or if you want to go somber we could find something black with some embroidered—"

"I need something turquoise," she said. "Fitted, to the knee. High neck, no sleeves."

From his chair, Magnus said, "But your injury—"

"Do you have something like that?"

Oona blinked. "I guess we can find one, if you're sure."

"Very sure. Thank you."

When Oona had gone, Magnus frowned at her. "What are you playing at?"

"Don't complain," she said. "Ethan might love it."

When the Americans showed an hour later, she and Magnus were already in the lobby of the hotel, and Ethan walked toward them amid so many clattering flashbulbs he looked like a marionette more than a man.

"Suyana," he said, the vowels slightly flattened as if by the sheer force of his presence.

She saw his open arms. He was going to embrace her.

She thought about the amount of information that crossed his desk; she thought about how easy it would be to get whatever she needed, if she was only willing to give up a little.

"Ethan," she said with a smile that felt almost real. She moved to meet him, so that when her arms went around him she'd be pressed against his chest.

The flashbulbs were a cacophony behind him. They could be kissing, she thought. From here, the cameras can't tell. (She thought, Should I kiss him? Does it matter, if no one sees?)

His shoulder scraped her wound.

After a moment, she steeled herself. Then she brushed her lips against his jaw, just under his mouth, like she'd gotten too shy at the last moment to really kiss him. She figured he liked them a little shy.

(Second kiss, she thought.)

He took in a breath, held it a moment too long.

"You almost died," he said, pulling back a little and frowning down at her.

She blinked. Either he was a mastermind, or he was in earnest. "So they say."

"If there's anything I can do, let me know." He looked solemnly at her for a moment before a smile crept across his face. "I'm still very interested in coming to an agreement."

"For their sake or for yours?"

Stupid question, she thought. Poor diplomacy. She regretted it the second it was out of her mouth. She should know better.

He did her the courtesy of not looking behind him in faux surprise at the trio of handlers lingering near the check-in desk. "I hear it could be to everyone's benefit," he said finally.

That was a diplomat's answer. And she was a diplomat; it had to be answer enough.

"You should walk me to my car, then," she said, slipping her arm in his. "And tell me where I'm meeting you for dinner."

"Oh, of course! What food do you like?"

Somewhere out of sight of Montmartre, she thought. "Surprise me."

He grinned down at her and covered her hand with his hand until the camera flashes blinded her, but her smile was armor, and it held.

In the greenroom, Oona zipped Suyana into her dress, and Suyana picked a pair of black pumps out of a lineup because the heels looked slightly like fangs, and by the time Magnus joined her, Oona was smoothing pomade over Suyana's loose hair.

"You don't want flyaways on TV," she said. "It's like having something in your teeth—that's all people will see. Trust me."

Suyana didn't doubt it.

"What will you do with it?" Magnus asked, taking a seat behind her. She watched him in the mirror as he took out his tablet and started work.

"Leave it," she said.

Oona took in a skeptical breath, which Suyana ignored, and Magnus looked up, which Suyana acknowledged by raising her eyebrows.

"They want a serious but innocent young woman making a comeback of character after an ordeal. You think a French roll is going to do that?"

Magnus looked at her a moment too long before he dropped his head back to his work. "We should talk about your speech."

"I know what I'm going to say."

He made a dubious noise, but his tablet chirped, and the noise turned into a circumspect hum. "The Americans have time to meet tomorrow," he said, grinning at the tablet. "How about that."

"We could meet for lunch in the dining room of the George V," Suyana suggested. "Since Ethan and I have nothing to hide, now."

Oona put something behind her ears that smelled like potpourri. Suyana let it go.

"We'll see," said Magnus. "I'm not sure you should be so anxious to be in public until you can look at him like you like him. The hotel was fine, but even Ethan's bound to catch on if you keep that smile glued on for hours."

Oona was pulling something out of a drawer and holding it up. "Just this, and you're done!"

"Is that a church bell?"

Oona sighed. "It's a statement piece."

The bracelet was a cuff of hammered brass so big it looked like a gauntlet as Oona clicked it shut around her wrist.

"No, thank you," said Suyana.

"It's very Native-Heritage," argued Oona.

"Not mine," said Suyana.

"It reminds them of your captivity," Magnus pointed out. "It's a strong statement."

She looked at his reflection in the mirror and snapped, "Then I shouldn't still be wearing a shackle, should I."

She and Magnus stared at each other in the mirror. (Something about the set of his face looked a little startled. Was today the first time he had ever believed her when she stood up for something?)

He must think it such a funny thing to take a stand over. Some bracelet.

But if she didn't have this fight with him now, it would

just delay something that had to happen sooner or later, if Suyana stood a chance of doing this without losing her mind. They might as well get it out of the way.

Oona looked back and forth, waiting for orders, until a PA knocked on the door and broke the silence.

"We're ready for you," he said.

Suyana looked at Magnus and raised her arm, shaking the cuff once. It was a test. Her, or them.

Magnus raised an eyebrow and said nothing.

Right, Suyana thought. Of course. For a moment she'd thought otherwise, but it was best to know before she took the stage how much she really was standing alone.

"I'm ready," she said.

She slid off the chair and moved for the door without looking behind her, heading for the stage as fast as she could. Halfway down the hall, Magnus caught up, and they walked in a tense silence all the way to the wings.

Suyana's speech was pressing on her, the sound of the crowd was pressing on her, and the idea that Magnus would still treat her like a liability felt like the flat of the knife on her back.

I could keep playing kind for a year, she thought. If I wanted to, I could lie to him with every look. By then either he or I will be gone—dead, or vanished, or back home—and this will all be over.

But something cold and ruthless turned inside her, and she thought: No.

Before she knew what she was doing, she'd turned to face him and advanced. He retreated before her, bemused, until he stumbled the last foot into the wall. She pinned him with her outstretched hand, her fingers curled in against the front of his jacket.

For the first time, she saw what he looked like when he feared her. (She'd killed a man. He shouldn't forget that. She couldn't.)

"A good man died to make way for you," she said. "If you want to pretend you're my ally then do as you please, and if you lie to me well enough that I buy it that's my fault, but don't think for a second I'm the person I was. I remember the list of enemies that I made as soon as that gun went off."

She leaned in an inch, drew back her lips to bare her teeth. "Don't be my enemy."

For three long breaths, he looked more nervous than she'd ever seen him. (Good, she thought.)

Then his eyes dropped to her arm—the crow's-feet going taut as he saw her wound—up to her mouth. His expression was strange; soft but sharpened, as if he had been listening to music and had finally recognized the song. He was shaking.

Suyana's fingertips went cold.

There was applause from the assembly, and Suyana stepped away, drew back her arm.

He was looking at her so strangely, for a moment, as if he was trying to decide what to apologize for. Then he pushed away from the wall with the graceful flat of his hand, and they took the last few steps to the edge of the curtain.

He was under control again, thanking the PA graciously, the tablet back in his hand as though he'd plucked it from the air, his expression as smooth and cool as ever.

Suyana kept her eyes on the stage, tried to put this in its place and not let it follow her now.

Magnus was a good handler; he didn't have to be a good man for that. If he feared her a little, it was in her favor. If they could keep away from open war, they were good enough at lying to look a little like allies.

He'll never be your ally, came the thought, thin and unwelcome and clouded as smoke, but some things couldn't be helped.

Margot stepped back from the mic, and Suyana realized she'd been announced, that this was it, that she was on.

"Suyana," Magnus said, so softly she hardly heard him. "I'm not your enemy."

She set her jaw. "Prove it," she said.

His expression shifted. Around her, he always found ways to look like a stranger.

She pulled off the bracelet, handed it to him without looking, and took the stage.

It was a long stage, and she took slow, even strides toward the podium, the black spikes of her shoes ringing like hammers.

A murmur rose from the crowd as they caught sight of the gunshot wound on her arm. Suyana measured her steps so the photos could capture it in all its sickly purple glory, the stretch marks a stark white web against her skin.

Walking across the stage, she was facing the Central Committee head-on. They were sitting calmly, trying not to look like the same people who'd agreed to cast her out.

All except Margot, who was looking at her the way a falcon looks at a snake, trying to decide if the fight is worth it.

Try me, Suyana thought. I'm listening to everything. See if you can catch me before I strike. Her shoulders were burning; she'd never been so ready for a fight.

For an instant, just before the stage lights hit her, Suyana could have sworn Margot was smiling.

When she reached the narrow podium she turned to face the crowd, cheated her right leg so the cameras could get the wound.

The photo pit was packed, and the chambers were standing room only. It looked like every country in the IA had turned out to see if what she had to say was up to scratch.

She let out a breath and took in the room. She marked Kipa, whose gaze was on her lap; she glanced down at Grace and Martine. Grace was giving Suyana a smile too small for anyone to catch; Martine wasn't looking at her at all.

Ethan was at the American's place; when she looked at him he smiled and nodded once, as if she'd been waiting for his encouragement.

When Suyana looked up at the mezzanine, she took only a moment to scan the audience. She didn't let herself linger on the shadows on the right where she thought she'd seen a familiar face. (Even from half a glance, she could tell that Daniel was concerned. He was welcome to be. She couldn't risk it.)

Her concern was how high she could stand tomorrow on the tower that she built tonight.

She cast one sidelong look at Magnus, who was still in the wings, watching her with a expression she couldn't quite meet. Then she leaned an inch into the mike.

"Ladies and gentlemen of the International Assembly," she said. "My name is Suyana Sapaki. I stand before you as the Face of my country, the United Amazonian Rainforest Confederation. I stand before you despite someone who would have killed me, rather than let me serve my homeland and her people."

There was a ripple of response in the gallery; she glanced

up at them just long enough for the volume of sympathetic outrage to rise.

"I stand before you," she said, one degree louder, keeping her tone even, "as someone who was a captive and now is free, someone condemned who is grateful for her life."

She cast a look around the chamber. Faces and handlers alike were silent, watching her.

"But, above all, I stand before you as a diplomat—a servant of her homeland, whose responsibility will not be severed even by death, and who rededicates herself here tonight to her country, to her people, and to the International Assembly, whose just cause is the bane of those who would do evil, and the pillar of those who would do right."

She'd debated resting so hard on the majesty of the IA— it wasn't as though she had much faith in them, and viewers at home were more interested in the gruesome details of her captivity than her political dedication. But she wasn't living among viewers at home; she wasn't even living in a country that was part of an uneasy whole. She was living alongside a Committee that had condemned her to die. They were the same people who were standing amid a deafening round of applause, calling her name.

She dropped her head in a pretense of humility. In her left periphery, Magnus was looking out at the crowd, his expression the closest to joy she'd ever seen on him. (That's what a diplomat with a future looked like.)

In her right periphery, Margot's hands were laced in her lap, so tense that her knuckles were white.

Suyana couldn't suppress a smile. More than the cameras clacking or the gallery above them going mad, those trembling hands meant Suyana had hit home.

Tomorrow offers for committee places would come in; Magnus would be arranging interviews. Tomorrow, it would be that much harder to make her disappear.

Suyana lifted her head, letting the applause go a moment longer before she continued with the promises and particulars that no one would really remember in the morning. It didn't matter. The Assembly and Chordata and the public had all seen what they needed to see; that was all they had to remember, for now. The rest would happen slowly as she climbed.

If it was a terrifying thing to think of, she didn't let herself tremble; if she glanced up at the gallery to find a familiar face, she didn't let herself linger.

She had people to impress, and there were cameras everywhere.

Suyana stood firmly at the center of the stage, looked out at the room, and began.

ACKNOWLEDGMENTS

As always, the number of people involved in the making of a book is significant, and I'm lucky to have had them. If this book has ended up in your hands, I owe thanks to everyone at Saga Press for their enthusiasm and dedication. In particular, I want to thank my editor, Navah, who was the first person to whom I ever mentioned this book (at a lunch too long ago to mention, with Ellen, whose eardrums we'll assume for dramatic clarity were slightly slower and heard it second) and who has been its champion ever since. Thanks to my former agent, Joe, who was the first to take an interest in it, and my agent, Barry, who has been an invaluable adviser and advocate. And deepest thanks to Stephanie, Kelly, Elizabeth, Alexa, and everyone who was endlessly generous with their time and comments in shaping this book from its earliest drafts, and whose support means so much.